Greetings from Nowhere

Greetings *from* NOWHERE

Barbara O'Connor

Frances Foster Books ⊘ Farrar, Straus and Giroux ⊘ New York

Copyright © 2008 by Barbara O'Connor
All rights reserved
Distributed in Canada by Douglas & McIntyre Ltd.
Printed in the United States of America
Designed by Irene Metaxatos
First edition, 2008
10 9 8 7 6 5 4 3 2 1

www.fsgkidsbooks.com

Library of Congress Cataloging-in-Publication Data
O'Connor, Barbara.
    Greetings from nowhere / Barbara O'Connor.— 1st ed.
        p. cm.
    Summary: In North Carolina's Great Smoky Mountains, a troubled boy and his
    mother, a happy family seeking adventure, a man and his lonely daughter, and the
    widow who must sell the run-down motel that has been her home for decades meet
    and are transformed by their shared experiences.
    ISBN-13: 978-0-374-39937-5
    ISBN-10: 0-374-39937-9
    [1. Hotels, motels, etc.—Fiction. 2. Interpersonal relations—Fiction. 3. Great
    Smoky Mountains (N.C. and Tenn.)—Fiction. 4. North Carolina—Fiction.] I. Title.

PZ7.O217Gre 2008
[Fic]—dc22
                                                                    2006037439

For Pool Girl

Greetings from Nowhere

"Harold would have known what to do," Aggie said to Ugly. She tossed the unopened envelope into the junk drawer on top of the batteries and rubber bands, old keys and more unopened envelopes.

"Let's go sit and ponder," Aggie said.

She scooped up the little black cat and shuffled across the dirty orange carpet. Years ago, the carpet had been thick and fluffy, but now it was thin and flat, with a path worn from the bed to the bathroom.

From the bathroom to the kitchenette.

From the kitchenette to the door.

Aggie pushed the screen door open and sat in the aluminum lawn chair outside Room 5. The cat looked up at her with his one eye, twitched his torn ear, and purred.

Aggie smiled.

"That is one ugly cat," Harold had said the day Ugly had strolled out of the woods and sat outside their door, meowing and carrying on something awful.

Aggie had never cared much for cats, but there was something about this one that was different. So she had fed him tuna fish and he had been there ever since.

"Okay, Ugly," Aggie said. "What should we ponder today?"

But Ugly just closed his eye and went to sleep, leaving Aggie to ponder alone.

She looked out at the road. Waves of heat floated up off the steamy asphalt. The air was thick and still. Every now and then a car whizzed by, making the Queen Anne's lace along the roadside bob and sway.

Aggie took a deep breath and let out a sigh that made Ugly stir a little on her lap. She could feel the empty lawn chair next to her, like something big and heavy and dark, pulling at her. And even though she didn't want to, she looked at it.

Harold's chair.

Harold's empty chair.

And then Aggie started to ponder how in the world Harold could be gone. One minute he had been here with her at the Sleepy Time Motel. And then the next minute . . .

Poof!

He was gone.

Just like that.

Keeled right over in the tomato garden without so much as a goodbye.

Then Aggie began to ponder what in the world she was going to do about all that mail in the junk drawer. Mail from the phone company and the electric company and the tax office.

Then she moved on to pondering how she was going to fix that clogged drain in Room 4 or what she was going to do about the wasp nest up under the eaves outside the office door.

And before long, Aggie felt so weighed down with sadness and worry that she couldn't stand to ponder another thing.

She picked up Ugly and went back inside.

She opened the blinds so her begonias could enjoy the noonday sun. Then she pushed aside the curtain that hung over the doorway between her room and the motel office.

"Maybe I should tidy up in there in case someone comes today and wants a room," she said to Ugly.

Aggie spent the whole afternoon tidying up the little office. She dusted the countertop. She straightened up the postcards on the rack by the door. She polished the little silver bell that guests rang to let her know they were there. She checked to make sure the room keys were in the right order on the cup hooks on the wall. Then she checked to see if the YES, WE'RE OPEN sign was still in the window.

She washed the coffee mugs she used for the free coffee. (That had been Harold's idea.) Then she straightened the stack of complimentary maps of the Great Smoky Mountains. (That had been her idea.)

"There," she said to Ugly. "Now we'll be ready if somebody comes."

But nobody came. Nobody had come for a long, long time. Nobody had come since . . . when? Aggie wondered. She flipped open the motel guest book and looked at the last entry. Nearly three months ago. Mr. and Mrs. R. J. Perry from Ocala, Florida. They had gotten lost on their way to Lake Junaluska and had been so tired they couldn't drive another mile.

Aggie had put them in the nicest room. Number 10. The corner room with three windows. Outside the door was a rocking chair that Harold's brother Frank had made out of tree branches.

The next morning, Aggie had given the Perrys free coffee and a complimentary map, and then they had left, and nobody had stayed at the motel since.

Aggie looked around the little office.

"There," she said again. "All tidy."

Aggie was surprised to notice it was already getting dark outside. She shivered as a cool mountain breeze drifted through the open windows. She took Harold's old brown sweater off the hook behind the door and slipped it on.

Then she used a red marker to put a big X through *May 22* on the wall calendar.

She had made it through another day.

Before she left the office, she flipped the switch that turned on the spotlight that lit up the Sleepy Time Motel sign.

The spotlight flickered once, twice, three times.

Then it went out.

Aggie shook her head. Harold would have fixed that old spotlight. He would have opened up his rusty toolbox and found just the right tool and gone straight out there and fixed it. Then the sign would have been all lit up for passersby to see.

SLEEPY TIME MOTEL
FREE COFFEE
COMPLIMENTARY MAP
VACANCY

But now the sign was dark.

And now Aggie knew what she had to do. She took a piece of paper out of the drawer.

For Sale, she wrote, and felt a jab in her heart.

Sleepy Time Motel. Shawnee Gap, North Carolina.

Another jab.

Ten lovely rooms with mountain view. Swimming pool. Tomato garden.

Jab, jab.

For sale by owners, Harold and Agnes Duncan.

Then she felt a jab that nearly knocked her over. Her hand trembled so much she could hardly keep the pen on the paper as she scratched out Harold's name.

She folded the paper, turned out the lamp, and pushed aside the curtain over the doorway.

"Come on, Ugly," she said.

She shuffled along the orange carpet pathway to the kitchenette to make some toast and warm milk.

Ugly blinked up at her.

She put the toast on the chipped plate that she and Harold had gotten as a wedding present all those years ago. She poured the milk into the china cup that had belonged to Harold's mother.

Then she sat at the little table by the window, listening to the ticking of the kitchen clock, the low hum of cars zooming up the interstate behind the motel, the croak of a bullfrog out in the woods somewhere.

She stared down at the dry toast. Every now and then she took a sip of the warm milk.

Finally, she got up and dumped the toast into Ugly's bowl. The bowl that had *Kitty* written on the side in red. The bowl that Harold had bought at a yard sale.

She poured the milk over the toast.

Ugly made little slurpy noises as he lapped up the mushy milk toast.

Then Aggie followed the orange carpet path over to the bed and lay down on top of the flowered bedspread, pulling Harold's old brown sweater snugly around her like a blanket.

Ugly sauntered over, licking his lips, and curled up on the pillow next to her.

Aggie watched the sun sinking lower and lower behind the mountains until the sky was totally dark. Then she closed her eyes and waited for another day.

Willow had an almost perfect life. She had her own room with a silky white bedspread. She had a collection of little china horses. And she had a friend named Maggie who loved to play with her china horses and was always very careful.

What she *didn't* have was two parents who loved each other.

Which is why her life was only *almost* perfect.

"We just don't love each other anymore," her father had said the day her mother left.

"But why not?" Willow had asked.

Her father hadn't answered. He had set his mouth into a

straight hard line that told Willow he had locked the door to his heart and thrown away the key.

When Grannie Dover came by, she said, "I knew Dorothy was trouble from day one."

Red splotches formed on Willow's father's neck and moved all the way up to his forehead.

"I don't want to hear that name in this house ever again," he said.

Grannie Dover lit a cigarette, tilted her chin up toward the ceiling, and blew out a thin stream of smoke. "Fine with me," she snapped.

But it wasn't fine with Willow.

She began to whisper her mother's name over and over inside her head.

Dorothy

Dorothy

Dorothy

She liked saying it so much, she decided she would say it a lot.

Just not out loud.

Sometimes, when her father was sleeping on the couch, Willow would tiptoe down the hall to his bedroom that used to be Dorothy's bedroom, too. She would peek in the drawers and on top of the closet shelf and under the bed, hoping to find a trace of her. Any little thing would do.

A shoe.

An earring.

A comb.

Anything.

But there was nothing. Her mother had taken every teeny tiny little thing. Sometimes Willow took the calendar off the kitchen wall and flipped back to March or April to look at her mother's writing there in the little squares.

Aunt Lurlene's birthday

Haircut 2 p.m.

Willow's school play

Willow would trace her mother's writing with her finger.

Up and around and down.

Up and around and down.

Most every afternoon, Willow lay on her bed and pressed her cheek against the cool, silky bedspread. Except for the thick, heavy heat and the steaming asphalt road out front, it didn't feel much like summer vacation. Sometimes her father went to work and sometimes he didn't. On the days he didn't, Willow wished he would take her swimming at the Y or let her make lemonade or set up the sprinkler for her and Maggie to run through.

Like Dorothy used to do.

But he didn't.

He just sat on the couch watching *Jeopardy!*, stroking the stubble of beard on his chin, and looking like the most miserable person on earth. His misery grew and grew until it filled up the whole house and seeped out of the doors and windows into the yard. It floated over the patch of weeds that used to be flowers that Dorothy grew. It circled the swing set where Willow used to play while Dorothy pinned wet sheets on the clothesline. And it snaked around the mailbox where Willow waited every morning at ten o'clock.

"Hello again, Willow," Juanita Lawson said when she pulled up in her rusty old station wagon to deliver the mail.

Willow heard the *I feel sorry for you* tone in Juanita's voice and saw the *aren't you pitiful* look on her face, so she kept her eyes on the ground when she reached for the mail. Then she dashed around back and sat on the steps and looked carefully at each envelope.

But there was never, not ever, anything from Dorothy.

So Willow took out her box of stationery with the roses around the edges and she wrote herself a letter.

Dear Willow,

How are you? I am fine. Do you miss me? I miss you. I have decided that I love your daddy, after all, so I am coming home.

See you soon.

> *Your loving mother,*
> *Dorothy*

Willow sealed the letter in the matching envelope and wrote on the front:

Miss Willow Dover
101 Lancaster Lane
Hailey, North Carolina

Then she rummaged through the drawer of the rickety table in the hall until she found a stamp.

The next day, she rode her bike to Hank's Quik Stop and dropped the letter into the mailbox out front.

Two days later, Juanita Lawson pulled up next to the Dovers' mailbox and said, "Ta-da!" as she thrust the rose-bordered envelope at Willow.

"I bet *this* is what you been waitin' for," she said.

Willow took the letter and ran around back and sat on the steps. She looked down at the envelope in her lap.

And then she got a bad, bad feeling because she realized she had been wrong.

You can fool a person.

You can fool a dog.

You can fool a cat or a horse or a teacher or a friend.

But you cannot ever fool a heart.

No matter how many letters from Dorothy she wrote, Willow's heart was still going to ache.

So she took the letter out to the patch of weeds that used to be flowers that Dorothy grew. She pushed the weeds aside and nestled the letter down in the middle where the sweet William and the gladiolus used to be.

Then she went inside and lay on her bed and wished everything were different.

Not all messed up like it was now.

Then, the very next day, Willow got her wish.

Sort of.

She sat at the kitchen table and poured milk on her cereal and watched her father's droopy face. He sipped coffee from a mug that said *Over the Hill* and read the morning paper. Suddenly, he slammed the cup down, sloshing coffee onto the table and making Willow jump.

He jabbed a finger at the paper and said, "That's it!"

"What?" Willow said.

He took a pen from his shirt pocket and circled something on the newspaper page.

"This is what I've been waiting for," he said, grinning down at the paper.

"What?" Willow asked again.

Her father began to pace, back and forth, from one side of the tiny kitchen to the other, muttering to himself and stroking his whiskery chin.

Willow cocked her head and tried to read what he had

circled on the newspaper. The only words she could read were the first two: *For Sale.*

"Are you gonna buy something, Daddy?" she said.

He stopped pacing and looked at Willow.

"Yes, I am," he said.

"What?"

"A new life."

"A new life?"

He nodded. "A new life."

Willow's stomach was starting to squeeze up and her heart was starting to thump. "But what about our old life?" she said.

Her father yanked the newspaper off the table.

"Our old life is history," he said.

"History?"

"History."

"So, is Dorothy history, too?" Willow asked in a tiny little voice because it felt scary saying *Dorothy* out loud like that.

Her father's face softened a bit, but he didn't say much of anything that Willow wanted to hear.

"I'm going to the bank," is what he said.

And then he added, "I think I'll shave."

When he left the room, Willow picked up the newspaper and read what he had circled:

FOR SALE: *Sleepy Time Motel. Shawnee Gap, North Carolina. Ten lovely rooms with mountain view. Swimming pool. Tomato garden. For sale by owner, Agnes Duncan.*

Willow felt a little ball of worry forming way down inside her. She went out back and sat in the middle of the weeds that used to be flowers that Dorothy grew. She closed her eyes and thought about her old life that was about to be history.

Then she said, "Dorothy. Dorothy. Dorothy," right out loud.

Loretta stared down at the package in her lap.

"Go on," her mother said. "Open it."

But Loretta wanted to hold on to that feeling just a little longer. That fluttery feeling in her stomach that came with wondering who in the world would send her a package and what in the world could it be.

She ran her hand over the wrinkled brown paper. She traced the twine with her finger. She studied the messy handwriting in blue ink.

Loretta Murphy
452 Jacob's Lane
Calhoun, Tennessee

That was her, all right.

Her name.

Her street.

Her town.

Her state.

She lifted the package and gave it a little shake next to her ear. Nothing rattled.

"Come on, Lulu," her mother said. "I'm dying to know what it is."

Loretta looked up at her mother.

"Who could have sent it?" she said.

Her mother put her arm around her. "You'll never know if you don't open it," she said, giving Loretta's shoulder a jiggle.

Loretta turned the package over and inspected the bottom of it. She lifted the twine and checked underneath.

No return address anywhere.

Just a postmark.

Henryville, IN

"What state is IN?" Loretta asked.

Her mother narrowed her eyes and tilted her chin up. "Hmmm. Indiana, I think," she said.

"Indiana," Loretta repeated softly.

"Okay, Lulu," her mother said. "I'll be in the kitchen. Call me when you open it."

She stood up with a grunt and shuffled into the kitchen, her denim shorts swish, swish, swishing.

Loretta looked down at the package again.

Slowly, she pulled the twine off one side. Then the other.

Slowly, she untaped the paper from the ends of the box.

Slowly, she took the paper off.

She opened the box.

Crumpled white tissue paper lay on top.

Loretta closed her eyes, took a deep breath, and lifted the tissue paper out of the box.

She opened her eyes.

Right on top was a note.

On yellow lined paper. Written in the same blue ink and the same messy handwriting as the address on the outside of the box.

Dear Loretta:

    Your mother passed on to the other side at 6:16 a.m. on June 6.

    She asked me to send you all her earthly possessions, enclosed herewith.

    She was a good person.

    She was my friend.

And that was all.

No name.

No goodbye.

Nothing.

Loretta felt a swirl of confusion.

Your mother?

What did that mean? Her mother was in the kitchen making deviled eggs.

Passed on to the other side?

What did that mean? The other side of *what*?

Loretta stared at the note and let the confusion swirl around her until it settled, like dust on the road.

And then she began to understand.

The mother in this note must be the one her parents called her *other mother*. The one who had carried her for nine months and given birth to her and surely loved her more than anything but wanted her to have a good life, not a hard life.

The mother Loretta had never known.

The mother Loretta *did* know was the one humming in the kitchen, making deviled eggs. The one who smelled like lavender talcum powder. The one who made doll clothes out of dishcloths and cradles out of oatmeal boxes. The one who called her Lulu and said to Loretta's father nearly every day, "Aren't we lucky, Marvin?"

Loretta nodded.

Yep. That was what *your mother* meant in this note.

But what about *passed on to the other side?*

Loretta felt her heart squeeze up.

"Mama?" she called into the kitchen.

She could see her mother at the kitchen counter, mashing egg yolks in one of her heavy yellow bowls with cherries on the side.

"Um, Mama?" she called a little louder.

Her mother came into the living room, wiping her hands on her apron. "What's the matter, Lulu?" she said.

Loretta showed her mother the note and waited.

The kitchen clock went *tick, tick, tick*.

Loretta's mother sat on the couch beside her and put her arm around her. Then she put her warm, soft cheek next to Loretta's and rocked.

Back and forth.

Back and forth.

Just like she had done when Loretta was little.

"This is a sad, sad day, Lulu," she said.

Now Loretta knew for sure what *passed on to the other side* meant.

Her other mother had died.

Loretta's insides felt all jumbled up. Like a jigsaw puzzle with too many pieces and nowhere to put them.

"I wonder who sent this," Loretta said.

Her mother stopped rocking and took Loretta's face in both her hands. "I don't know," she said, shaking her head.

They sat quietly for a while, both of them staring down at the box in Loretta's lap. Outside the open window behind them, the sprinkler sputtered in circles in the front yard.

Across the street, some kids were playing. Laughing. Hollering. Someone called, "Not it!"

Loretta took the things out of the box and laid them out on the coffee table, one by one.

A tattered pincushion shaped like a lady's high-heeled shoe.

A Japanese fan with white flowers and a tassel of silky red ribbon.

A tarnished silver pocket watch engraved with the initials *WKL*.

A picture of a hummingbird torn from a magazine.

A white leather Bible.

Tiny scissors shaped like a bird.

A sparkly poodle dog pin.

A pale blue handkerchief with the letter *P* embroidered in pink.

A heart-shaped box made of red velvet.

And a silver charm bracelet.

"Aren't those some nice treasures," Loretta's mother said.

Loretta nodded. She couldn't take her eyes off all those things. She picked them up one at a time, turning them over and over.

Feeling them.

Smelling them.

She fingered the lacy edges of the handkerchief. She leafed through the Bible pages. She opened and closed the

Japanese fan. She took the lid off the heart-shaped box. Inside was a photograph. A creased and faded photograph of a young girl. A girl about ten or eleven. A girl about Loretta's age. The girl stood on a rock in the middle of a creek, wearing a red-checkered bathing suit and holding a towel in one hand.

Her legs were bowed and skinny.

Like Loretta's.

Her hair was straight and dark.

Like Loretta's.

"This is her," Loretta whispered.

She stared down at the photograph. She wished she could do magic. *Abracadabra* and *poof*! The girl in the photograph would come to life, jumping off the rock and right into Loretta's living room. She would sit on the floor across from them and tell them all about herself.

"How'd she know where I live?" Loretta asked.

Her mother shook her head. "I don't know, Lulu," she said.

Loretta studied the charm bracelet.

"Look at these," she said, holding the bracelet up so the charms dangled in front of them.

She examined each tiny charm.

A cowboy boot.

A starfish.

A barrel with *Niagara Falls* engraved on the side.

Mickey Mouse.

A map of Vermont.

A bear holding a little sign that said *Great Smoky Mountains*.

A palm tree.

The Statue of Liberty.

A cactus.

"I wonder what she was like," Loretta said, laying the bracelet out on the coffee table.

Her mother put her soft, plump hand on Loretta's knee. "I bet she was just like you," she said. "Sweet and smart and funny and—"

Her mother snapped her fingers. "Hey, wait a minute . . ."

Loretta studied her mother's face. "What?" she said.

"I bet those charms are *places*!"

"Places?"

"Yeah, you know, special places. I bet those are places she visited."

Loretta looked down at the bracelet. "Really?"

Her mother nodded. "Sure," she said. "I bet you anything. You know how people get charms that mean something special to them. And look at all those." She nodded toward the bracelet. "Every single one of them is something that comes from a *place*."

"Oh, yeah," Loretta said. "Like maybe that boot's from Texas."

"And that cactus might be from Arizona," her mother said.

"What about the starfish?" Loretta said. "Florida maybe?"

"Maybe."

"She sure went to a lot of places, didn't she?"

"She sure did."

Loretta put all her other mother's earthly possessions back into the box. She covered them with the tissue paper and put the lid on. She smoothed out the wrinkled brown paper with the palm of her hand and folded it into a small square.

She put both hands on top of the box in her lap and listened to the sputter of the sprinkler in the yard.

The slow, steady breathing of her mother next to her.

The tinkly music of an ice cream truck way off in the distance somewhere.

Then she opened the box, took out all her other mother's earthly possessions, and studied them one by one all over again.

❧ ❧ ❧

When Loretta's father came home, she showed him the box. She read him the note. She took out each thing and put it on the coffee table in front of him. She showed him the photograph of the girl on the rock.

Her father pursed his lips and nodded.

Then he cupped his warm, rough hand around the back of her neck.

The kitchen clock went *tick, tick, tick.*

"Well, now," he finally said.

"Mama and I think those charms are from places she visited," Loretta said. "Do you think so?"

"I reckon that might be true," he said, giving the back of Loretta's neck a little squeeze.

Loretta put all the things back into the box. The smell of fried chicken drifted out of the kitchen.

"I wonder what she was like," Loretta said.

Her father took his baseball cap off and scratched his head.

That night at the dinner table, they talked about the charm bracelet, trying to guess where each charm had come from. Wondering out loud which place Loretta's other mother had liked best.

And then Loretta said it again.

"I wonder what she was like."

The kitchen clock went *tick, tick, tick.*

Suddenly her father slapped his hand on the table. "I have an idea," he said.

"What?" Loretta said.

"Why don't we visit some of those places on that charm bracelet?" Loretta's father grinned at them.

Loretta felt her heart leap with excitement.

"Really?"

Her father wiped his mouth with a paper napkin and nodded. "Sure," he said.

Loretta cocked her head and raised her eyebrows. "Texas?" she said.

Her father scratched his chin. "Hmmm," he said. "That's a little far. Why don't we start closer to home?"

"What about the Smoky Mountains?" Loretta's mother said.

Loretta crossed her fingers under the table and waited, watching her father's face.

He squinted up at the ceiling. Then he slapped his hand on the table again. "Sure!" he said. "Let's do it."

Loretta ran and got the charm bracelet. She held it over the dinner table so the tiny silver bear dangled in front of them.

The silver bear from the Great Smoky Mountains.

Then she hugged her father and kissed her mother and said, "Thank you."

The kitchen clock went *tick, tick, tick.*

And Loretta's mother said, "Aren't we lucky, Marvin?"

Kirby Tanner snatched a package of red licorice off the shelf beside the cash register and jammed it into his pocket. He glanced out the front window of the gas station to make sure the old man was still pumping gas, then he took a piece of bubble gum out of the jar on the counter. He unwrapped it, tossed the wrapper on the floor, and popped the gum into his mouth. Then he headed out to the car to wait for his mother.

"Where y'all from?" the old man asked, wiping his hands with an oily cloth.

Kirby didn't answer. He climbed into the front seat of the car and stared straight ahead.

"I *said*, where y'all from?" The old man peered through the window at Kirby.

Kirby took his sneakers off and tossed them onto the floor with all the other junk down there. An empty soda can. A McDonald's wrapper. Cigarette butts. The tattered shoebox that Burla Davis had given him, tied up with string.

"Just some little ole things I thought you might like," Burla had said that day Kirby had gone over to say goodbye.

Had it been only yesterday?

Kirby could feel the licorice in the pocket of his shorts. It felt hot, like fire, burning through the thin cotton.

When he heard his mother's sandals slapping on the concrete, he looked up. She had pinned her frizzy red hair on top of her head and was wiping her neck with a paper towel.

"Great day for the AC to go out on this piece of junk," she said, giving the tire of their car a kick.

The old man chuckled. "I hear ya," he said. "Want me to take a look at it?"

"You gonna fix it for free?" she said.

"Can't do that," the man said. "I could give you a good deal, though."

Kirby's mother yanked the car door open and flopped inside, tossing her purse into the backseat.

"Yeah, I bet," she muttered, slamming the door shut and starting the engine with a roar.

The tires kicked up sand and gravel as Kirby and his

mother sped out of the gas station and back onto the highway. Thick, hot air whipped through the open windows, blowing paper napkins and empty cigarette packs around the car.

Kirby leaned against the door and put his face out the window, letting the wind blow his hair back off his forehead. He stared at his reflection in the side mirror.

He looked mean.

No, maybe he didn't.

Maybe he just *felt* mean.

Mean? No, not mean.

Mad? Yeah. Mad.

Kirby felt mad and he looked mad.

No wonder everybody hated him.

His mother lit a cigarette. "Get your feet off the dash," she said, swatting his legs.

"How much farther?" Kirby kept watching his mad face in the mirror.

He felt his mother's eyes on him. "I still don't know why I had to be the one to drive you up here," she said. "Seems like your sorry excuse for a father could make an effort to do something useful once in a while."

Kirby took the licorice out of his pocket and tossed it out the window.

"You know, Kirby," his mother said, "this is your last chance to straighten up and fly right."

Kirby glared at his reflection in the mirror. He hated those freckles. He hated that red hair.

"If this school don't whip you into shape, I'm through." His mother blew a stream of cigarette smoke up to the roof of the car. "You mess up this time," she said, "you ain't coming back to *my* house."

Kirby took the gum out of his mouth and stuck it on the mirror, right in the middle of his reflection.

"Virgil don't need this drama every minute of the day, neither," his mother said.

Kirby made a little snorting sound when she said that about his stepfather. He knew that would make her mad, but he didn't care. He wanted her to be mad. It was her own fault she had to go and marry an old man like Virgil who was sick in bed all the time, so now she had to work two jobs and come home tired every night.

"And Ace," his mother went on. "How do you think Ace feels about you? Every time you pull one of your stunts at school, you humiliate him."

Yeah, right, Kirby thought. Perfect little brother Ace. Mama's precious lamb.

"You know, Dr. Lawton said flat out that Ace's bedwetting problem is 'cause of you." His mother flicked her cigarette out the window.

The air blowing through the car was getting cooler as the road took them farther up the mountain. Every now and then, Kirby could see a creek through the trees below them. He wished they would stop and wade in it. Or maybe sit at a picnic table and eat bologna sandwiches and drink Kool-Aid.

Play checkers.

Be nice to each other.

But they didn't stop. They kept right on going. Farther and farther from home. Closer and closer to Smoky Mountain Boys' Academy.

A bad-boy school, Ace called it.

Last stop before prison, Virgil called it.

Total disciplinary environment, the brochure called it. *Nestled in the heart of the beautiful Smoky Mountains. Strict but loving atmosphere.*

When Kirby had gone next door to show the brochure to Burla Davis, she'd said, "Why, I think this place looks real nice, Kirby. I bet you're gonna love it there."

She had pointed to the pictures inside the brochure. Boys building birdhouses in a woodwork shop. Boys playing football. Boys sitting all happy and smiling in a classroom.

"This'll be a fresh start, Kirby," Burla said.

Then she set out a plate of those tiny little doughnuts Kirby loved. When it started to get dark outside, Burla hadn't told him to go home. She never did. She always let him sit at her cracked Formica table in her kitchen with the teapot wallpaper, and she never told him to go home. Not even when he stuck gum up under her kitchen chairs or made little mountains of salt on the counter. Not even when he said cuss words right out loud in front of her.

"I've lived a long time, Kirby," she always said. "I've heard all them words before."

Kirby's thoughts were interrupted by a whirring, grinding, clanking noise as the car began to jerk and sputter.

His mother threw her hands up in the air.

"Oh, great," she said. "Just what I need."

Sputter. Rattle. Clank.

She pulled the car to the side of the road. Black smoke drifted out of the tailpipe and floated in the air beside them.

His mother banged the steering wheel with her fist.

"I *told* that no-account father of yours this piece of junk wouldn't make it," she hollered at Kirby.

"What're we gonna do?" Kirby said.

His mother dropped her head back against the seat and closed her eyes.

"Kirby," she said. "Do I look like the person who wrote *The Answer Book of Life*?"

"No, ma'am." Kirby was surprised to hear his own voice sound so small and pitiful. He had been trying hard to act like he didn't care that he was going to that school. Now his voice was about to go and give him away. But then, his mother probably wouldn't notice anyway.

"How should I know what we're gonna do?" His mother jerked the door open and got out.

The car rattled, then let out one big cough before the engine died.

Kirby got out of the car. The ground felt cool and sandy beneath his bare feet. From way down in the gulley below them came the faint sound of flowing water.

"Must be a creek down there," he said.

His mother walked around the car, glaring at it.

"Maybe we should flag somebody down," Kirby said, looking up one side of the road and down the other.

His mother yanked the car door open and fumbled through the glove box. She took out a tattered map and spread it out on the hood.

"I don't even know where we are," she said, squinting down at the map. She traced a squiggly line with her long red fingernail. "Bird's Creek ain't even on this map," she said. "The lady at that school said it was off Highway 15 near Bird's Creek."

Kirby wandered to the edge of the woods. Soft green ferns rippled in the breeze. He ran his toe over the carpet of moss beneath the trees. He wouldn't ever admit it out loud, but he was beginning to think it was kind of nice up here in the mountains.

Cool and moist and green.

Not like the hot, red-dirt yard back home.

"Come on," his mother called. She climbed into the car and turned the key. The engine whirred and chugged, sending more puffs of black smoke into the air. "Get in, quick," she hollered, "before this piece of junk dies again."

As they sputtered up the winding mountain road, Kirby practiced pig Latin in his head.

Upid-stay.

It-nay it-way.

Ut-shay our-yay ap-tray.

All the words that made Ace run crying to Mama.

"Come on, you big piece of junk." His mother pounded the steering wheel. "Don't stop now."

But that big piece of junk didn't listen to her.

It stopped.

Pow.

Rattle.

Thunk.

Hiss.

Silence.

Before Kirby could say a word, his mother was out of the car and storming off up the side of the road, her hands clenched into tight fists at the ends of her stiff, skinny arms. Her sandals kicked up little pebbles, leaving a cloudy trail of dust behind her.

Kirby got out and hollered to her. "Where you going?"

But she didn't answer. Didn't stop. Didn't even slow down.

"What about all my stuff?" Kirby called.

Finally she stopped. She flopped down in the weeds on the side of the road and put her head on her knees.

"You want your purse?" Kirby said.

Her shoulders shook. She must have been crying, but Kirby couldn't hear her.

He felt a wave of mad wash over him. Why was *she* crying? *She* wasn't the one everybody treated like dirt. *She* wasn't the one being sent away 'cause nobody wanted her around anymore.

He reached into the backseat, grabbed his mother's purse, and hurled it in her direction. It hit the ground and burst open, sending lipstick and pens and gum skidding out into the middle of the road.

His mother jumped up and said some nasty things as she gathered her stuff up and jammed it back into her purse.

She shot Kirby a glare and then marched off up the side of the road, her sandals slap, slap, slapping.

Her arms pumping.

Her purse swinging.

Kirby opened the car door and took Burla's box off the floor. He jammed it into his duffel bag and slammed the car door shut—hard—sending an echo down the side of the mountain.

Then he headed up the road after his mother.

Aggie pushed her fork through her cold scrambled eggs.

Back and forth.

Around and around.

And back and forth again.

Then she sighed.

A great big shoulder-heaving sigh.

"Here, Ugly," she said.

She scraped the eggs into Ugly's bowl and set her plate on top of the other dirty dishes in the sink. "I never did like eggs much, anyway," she said.

She pulled back the faded yellow curtains and peered through the dusty window screen. The sun was already high over the mountains. A smoky blue haze hovered in the air along the tops of the trees.

"Maybe I should call that man back and tell him I've changed my mind," she said to Ugly. "Maybe I should talk to Arnie Becker over at the bank. He could lend me some money and I could . . ." Her voice trailed off.

The room grew quiet.

Ugly's tail twitched back and forth on the floor as he licked the last speck of egg out of his *Kitty* bowl.

He looked up at Aggie and blinked his eye.

"Yeah, I know," Aggie said. "That bank idea probably isn't a good one."

Aggie watched the birds hop around the small patch of grass out back. Every now and then, one of them fluttered up to the bird feeder, then back down to the grassy patch.

"That feeder's empty," Aggie said. "I wonder when that happened."

She shuffled along the worn carpet path from the kitchenette to the door and peered outside at the gravel parking lot. The weeds had gotten so tall, she could hardly see the swimming pool from her door anymore. Some of the weeds were blooming into colorful wildflowers, which Aggie kind of liked.

"Maybe I'll just leave it like that," she said. "What do you think, Ugly?"

Ugly sat in a square of sunlight in the middle of the room, cleaning his patchy black fur.

"I guess I better get a room ready for that man." Aggie looked at Ugly. "What was his name?"

Ugly jumped onto the back of Harold's old lounge chair and curled up on the crocheted afghan folded there.

Aggie went to the bedside table and squinted down at the notepad by the phone. She adjusted her glasses. "Dover," she said. "Clyde Dover."

At first, she had felt a big weight lifted when Clyde Dover had called to say he wanted to buy the motel. He had been so convincing, telling her how he didn't even need to see it. How he just knew he was gonna love it. How he was gonna do all kinds of things to attract the tourists who zipped by down there on the interstate. He had made her think she would be doing just the right thing by signing all those papers he was sending in the mail. Those papers that would make the sale of the motel go quicker.

"All we need is an inspection and—*bingo*. Done," he'd said.

But now, well, now Aggie wasn't so sure.

Maybe she shouldn't have signed those papers, after all.

"Harold would have known what to do," she said, taking the bucket off the hook on the wall of the kitchenette.

She checked to make sure all the cleaning supplies were inside it. Then she went in the office and got the key to Room 10.

"Come on, Ugly," she said.

She hadn't been in that room since the Perrys from Ocala, Florida, had left. When she opened the door, a musty odor drifted out.

She opened the windows and fluffed the pillows and smoothed the bedspread. She dusted the dresser and cleaned the mirror and straightened the painting over the bed. *Waterfall in Summer.*

Waterfall in Winter was hanging in Room 4, but Aggie liked this one better.

She cleaned the bathroom sink and refolded the towels and made sure there was extra soap. Those tiny little bars of soap with the wrappers that had *Sleepy Time Motel* printed in shiny gold letters.

Then she went outside and sat in the chair by the door and wished her back didn't hurt so bad.

She listened to the echoey roar of the trucks down on the interstate behind the motel.

She watched Ugly cleaning himself out by the flagpole.

"I wonder where Harold put that flag," she said out loud to nobody.

She buttoned Harold's old brown sweater and let her heavy eyelids close. Before long, her chin dropped against her chest and she slept.

She dreamed about Harold. He was young and strong and handsome, wearing his army uniform and dancing the jitterbug in her parents' front parlor.

Willow stared out the back window of the pickup truck, watching her old life get smaller and smaller until it began to disappear.

The little brick house with the screened porch was gone.

The swing set was gone.

The clothesline was gone.

The weed-filled garden was gone.

She turned around and stared out the front window.

"What if I don't like our new life?" she said.

Her father sighed. That little vein on the side of his forehead twitched. "Willow," he said in that voice Willow hated, "you'll like it, okay?"

"But what if I don't?"

Willow looked down at her shoes. The pink plastic sandals that Dorothy had bought. They were getting too small. They were starting to hurt her feet. But Willow didn't care. She loved wearing them anyway.

Her father turned the radio on. That little vein twitched again.

Willow watched more and more pieces of her old life disappear as she and her father headed out of town.

The Triangle Drugstore.

The Hailey Fire Department.

The Elks Lodge.

She mouthed "Goodbye" as they passed each one.

Before long, there was nothing left of her old life at all.

Every now and then, Willow looked down at her hands. Touched her arms. Felt her hair. Just to make sure she wasn't disappearing, too.

But she wasn't. She stayed right there in the front seat of her father's red pickup truck, speeding along the highway toward the mountains. The back of the truck was piled high with boxes and covered with a bright blue tarp. One of the boxes had *Willow* written on the side in black marker. Inside the box were Willow's clothes, her china horses, some books, and the calendar with Dorothy's writing in the little squares of April.

They stopped for lunch at the Waffle House off Interstate 40. Willow's father studied a map while Willow ate waffles with butter. No syrup. The same way Dorothy ate waffles. Willow wondered if her father noticed.

Probably not.

"What if we don't like that motel?" she asked him.

He didn't look up from the map. "We'll like it," he said.

"But what if we don't?"

Her father traced along the roads on the map with a pen. "Then we'll look for another motel," he said.

"Oh." Willow's shoulders slumped.

She was going to hate living in a motel. She was sure about that. Who ever heard of a kid living in a motel? How could you say to your best friend, "Come over to my motel to play"?

But then, she probably wouldn't have a best friend. She probably wouldn't have *any* friends. She definitely wouldn't have a friend like Maggie.

Late that afternoon, they turned off the interstate onto a narrow mountain road that twisted back and forth and around and around the mountain. Every now and then, there was a clearing and Willow could look out at the gray-green treetops below. Once in a while, they passed a store. Brightly colored signs announced the things inside.

BOILED PEANUTS.

INDIAN BLANKETS.

PEACH PRESERVES.

Before long, there were no more stores, no more signs, no

more cars. Just a few lonely-looking houses with sleeping dogs in the yards and old men on the porches. A few trailers, nestled in among the trees at the end of dirt driveways.

Willow stared glumly out the window.

She was a long, long way from her little brick house in Hailey.

From the winding driveway where she and Maggie played jump rope.

From the bedroom with her china horse collection lined up on the white shelf over the bed.

From the vine-covered mailbox that never had letters from Dorothy.

Willow's old life was history.

Loretta

"Smell that air," Loretta's mother said, closing her eyes and taking a deep breath. "I just love the Smoky Mountains."

"Me too," Loretta said.

She had never been to the Smoky Mountains before. She had known they were there, of course, starting way over on the other side of Tennessee from where she lived and stretching clear on into North Carolina. She had made a model of them one time for school, mixing up a goopy clay out of flour and salt and water and patting it into mounds on cardboard. She had painted the mountains green and brown.

Now here she was in the *real* Smoky Mountains, sitting in

the backseat of their big white van with *Murphy's Heating and Plumbing* painted on the side. Her father's tools slid back and forth across the metal floor of the van as they followed the winding road up the mountain.

Every few minutes, Loretta wiggled her hand, making the silver charm bracelet jingle on her wrist. She had looked at each charm about a million times, imagining the place it had come from.

The cowboy boot from Texas.

The starfish from Florida.

The cactus from Arizona.

She felt a tingle of excitement as she looked out the window at the sights along the roadside. Souvenir shops and country stores. Vegetable stands and flea markets.

When they crossed the state line, they stopped to take pictures, posing beside the WELCOME TO NORTH CAROLINA sign, their arms around each other, smiling and saying "Cheese."

They ate sandwiches at a picnic table on the side of the road.

"Listen how quiet it is," Loretta's mother said. They all three sat still, cocking their heads and looking skyward, taking in the silence that was interrupted only by the bees buzzing around the tops of their soda cans.

Every once in a while, a car went by. Luggage piled on the top. Bicycles hanging on racks off the back.

Loretta's mother took a folded piece of paper out of her back pocket and opened it up on the picnic table.

"Maybe tonight we can decide where we wanna go first," she said.

They had made a list of the places they wanted to visit in the Smoky Mountains.

Maggie Valley
Cherokee
Santa's Land Theme Park
Cades Cove
Tuckaleechee Caverns
Clingmans Dome
Dollywood

Loretta's father had said they probably couldn't get to all those places on this trip, but maybe they could come back some other time.

Maybe this time Loretta would have to choose between Santa's Land and Dollywood, he said.

Loretta wished she knew exactly where her other mother had gone when *she* was in the Smoky Mountains.

When they packed up their picnic stuff and loaded the cooler back into the van, Loretta's father took his cap off and stretched. "I'm just about ready to call it a day," he said.

So they kept their eyes open for a motel.

Loretta wondered where her other mother had stayed when *she* was in the Smoky Mountains.

As they got higher and higher into the mountains, the sun got lower and lower in the sky. They passed more souvenir shops and vegetable stands, but not a single motel.

"We might have to go back down to the interstate if we don't find something soon," Loretta's father said.

"We'll find something," Loretta's mother said. "Keep your peepers peeped, Lulu."

So Loretta rolled down the window and leaned out, letting the cool mountain air blow her bangs off her forehead, and kept her peepers peeped.

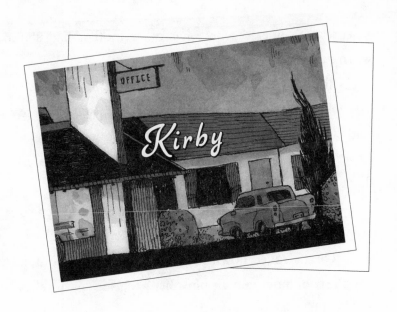

Kirby's mother rang the bell on the counter again.

"Well, this is just great," she said. "Nobody's here."

The postcard rack squeaked as Kirby spun it around and around.

"Stop it, Kirby," his mother hollered. "I've got a splittin' headache. My feet are killin' me. And I need a cigarette."

She slammed her hand down on the bell again.

Three times.

Ding. Ding. Ding.

"I'm going to go look for somebody," she said, shoving the screen door open.

Kirby strolled around the office, running his hand along the walls, shuffling through the maps on the counter, turning the pages of the guest book. He studied the postcards in the rack by the door. Pictures of mountains. Indians. Bears. He picked one that said *Greetings from the Great Smoky Mountains*, folded it in half, and stuffed it into his pocket.

He went behind the counter and studied the calendar with the red X's through the days. He jiggled the keys hanging on cup hooks on the wall.

He peered into the room behind the curtain. It was jammed with furniture. A bed. A tattered lounge chair. Tables. Bureaus. In one corner of the room was a little kitchen. The sink was filled with dishes. The countertop was cluttered with milk cartons, paper towels, and cans of cat food. On the floor under a tiny round table was a bowl with *Kitty* on the side. Flowerpots filled with drooping, pink-flowered plants lined the windowsills.

Kirby went to the front of the office and hopped over his duffel bag. Then back again. Then over again. Then back again.

Hop.

Hop.

Hop.

Hop.

Meow.

Kirby stopped hopping.

A scruffy black cat with one eye sat outside the screen door.

Kirby pushed the door open. The cat strolled inside and rubbed against Kirby's legs, purring.

Kirby sat on his duffel bag and held his hand out. The cat sniffed it, his nose twitching and his scraggly tail swishing back and forth on the floor.

Then the cat jumped right into Kirby's lap.

"What happened to your ear, fella?" Kirby said, running his finger along the cat's torn ear. "And your eye?"

The cat rubbed his face against Kirby's shoulder and purred again.

"I bet you been in a fight," Kirby said.

The cat blinked.

"A lot of fights," Kirby said.

He scratched the cat's neck.

"I guess nobody likes you," he said.

The cat looked up at Kirby and let out a tiny little *meow*.

"Yeah," Kirby said, "I know how you feel."

"Hello?"

A voice drifted into Aggie's dream.

"Hello?"

There it was again.

Aggie opened her eyes and sat up. Her neck ached. She blinked, adjusting her eyes to the afternoon sun.

"Hello?" came the voice again. And then a woman appeared, walking from the direction of the office. A wild-haired woman in short shorts and flapping sandals.

Aggie stood up, forgetting about the bucket in her lap. It hit the concrete with a clatter and rolled, sending sponges and brushes and spray bottles scattering into the gravel parking lot.

"Is this place open?" the woman said.

Aggie straightened her glasses and smoothed her hair. "Yes, ma'am," she said. "It is."

"I need a room," the woman said. Her red hair framed her face in frizzy curls. She smelled like cigarettes.

For one tiny little moment, Aggie thought about saying, "No smoking, okay?"

That's what Harold would have said.

But she didn't.

She gathered up the cleaning supplies and said, "Let's go over to the office and I'll fix you right up."

Aggie led the way up the sidewalk to the office. She opened the screen door and jumped, startled. A young boy was sitting on a duffel bag with Ugly in his lap. He had the same red hair, the same freckled white skin as the woman.

"For cryin' out loud, Kirby!" the woman hollered. "Get outta the way."

Ugly jumped off the boy's lap and darted around behind the counter.

"Ugly must like you," Aggie said to the boy. "He's usually kinda shy."

"Really?" the boy said.

Aggie nodded. "Shoot," she said, "he didn't sit on my lap till I fed him about a hundred cans of tuna."

Aggie turned to the woman. "I'm Agnes Duncan," she said. "But you can call me Aggie."

"I'm Darlene Tanner," the woman said. "That's my son, Kirby," she added, jerking her head toward the boy.

"Nice to meet you." Aggie smiled at them, but they didn't smile back. The woman was rifling through her purse. The boy was glaring at the floor.

"Well, now," Aggie said. "If you'll just sign that guest book, I'll get you the key."

Which room should she give them? Aggie wondered. Room 7? That one was closer to the ice machine.

But did that ice machine still work? Aggie couldn't remember.

Maybe Room 1. That was the other corner room.

Yes, that was it. Room 1.

"There's free coffee in the morning," she said. "And here's your complimentary map of the Great Smoky Mountains."

The woman took the map. "Oh, good," she said. "I can use this. I need to get to Smoky Mountain Boys' Academy. Near Bird's Creek off Highway 15. How far is that?"

"Bird's Creek is just a few miles up thataways." Aggie flung her arm toward the road.

"How do you get there?" the woman asked.

Aggie looked up at the ceiling. "Hmmm," she said. "I couldn't really tell you. I don't drive much anymore, and, well, things have changed so much around here over the years . . ."

Truth was, Aggie didn't drive at all anymore. She hadn't

renewed her driver's license when it had expired almost eight years ago. Harold had been so good at driving.

The woman said a cuss word and Aggie thought "My, my" to herself but didn't say it out loud.

She looked over at the boy and wondered if he had heard the cuss word. He was still glaring at the floor like he could burn a hole right through the linoleum with his eyes. Through the linoleum and clear on down into the red clay earth beneath.

"I hope Kirby won't mind sleeping on a cot," Aggie said. "It's a little lumpy, but it's right big. It's in the closet, okay?"

The woman didn't answer. She told the boy to get his bag and come on.

Aggie was surprised how easily such a scrawny kid picked up that heavy-looking bag.

"Y'all got a car?" Aggie said, glancing around the parking lot as she led them up the walk to Room 1.

"A big piece of junk on the side of the road," the woman said.

"Oh, well," Aggie said. "You've come to the right place if you got car trouble 'cause Harold . . ."

Aggie clutched her heart. How long was it going to take for her to realize that Harold was gone?

Forever?

Probably.

Probably forever.

"Um, never mind," she said, unlocking the door to the room. "How long are y'all planning on staying?"

"Not long," the woman said. "Just till I can get that wreck of a car fixed so I can get Kirby on up to that school."

Then the woman and her son went inside Room 1 and closed the door without so much as a thank you.

Aggie went back to the office and looked at the guest book.

Darlene and Kirby Tanner; Fountain Inn, South Carolina.

Wasn't it nice to see new names there on the line below the Perrys from Ocala, Florida?

Maybe things were going to pick up after all, she thought. Maybe Darlene and Kirby would stay for a while and then she could pay the phone bill and the electric bill. Maybe she should tell that man Clyde Dover the Sleepy Time Motel wasn't for sale, after all.

Willow's father stopped the truck.

"There it is," he said.

"That?" Willow stared out the window at the motel. It looked deserted, like no one had been there in a long time. The sign out front was faded and peeling. Wildflowers grew in the gravel parking lot. The swimming pool was empty, weeds poking out of the cracked concrete.

Willow's father pulled the truck into the parking lot. The tires made a crunching noise on the gravel that seemed to echo clear across the mountain. When he turned the engine off, silence fell over them, thick and heavy.

Willow counted the rooms of the motel. Ten. Only ten

rooms in the whole motel. Five on one side. Five on the other side.

Right in the middle was a screen door with a crooked, handwritten sign.

OFFICE.

In the window next to the door was another sign.

YES, WE'RE OPEN.

Rickety-looking lawn chairs sat outside the door of each room. A black cat was curled up in one of them.

"Wait here," Willow's father said, heading for the office.

"Hello?" her father called through the screen door.

Silence.

"Hello?" he called again.

Silence.

He opened the door and disappeared inside. A few minutes later, he came back out.

"It looks like no one's here," he said.

Good, Willow thought.

"Mr. Dover?" someone called from the door.

A tiny old woman in bedroom slippers shuffled toward them. Her faded brown sweater hung clear down to her knees.

"Are you Mr. Dover?" she said.

Before Willow's father could answer, the old woman said, "I'm Agnes Duncan. But you can call me Aggie."

She tucked a wisp of thin gray hair behind her ear. "I've got your room ready." She nodded toward the far corner of the motel. Her face was lined and leathery, but her eyes were clear and sparkly. She kept pushing the stretched sleeves of her sweater up over her bony elbows.

Willow watched from the front seat of the truck as her father glanced around the weed-filled parking lot. Squinted out at the cracked, empty swimming pool. Frowned over at the faded, peeling sign.

"I know it ain't much to look at now," Aggie said. "But you shoulda seen it in its heyday." She gestured with her skinny arm, making the sweater flop down over her hand. "This whole parking lot was filled to overflowing. Cars and kids and all. Guests in every room every night. Well, almost every night . . . at least in the summer . . . And—"

"Mrs. Duncan, I—"

"Aggie," she said. "Please. Call me Aggie."

She squinted over at the pickup truck where Willow sat.

Willow slumped down in the seat.

"Is that your girl?" Aggie said.

"Yes," her father said. "That's Willow."

"Willow!" Aggie grinned. "Well, what a fine name!" She waved toward the truck. "Hello, Willow," she called.

Willow waved back.

A tiny little wave.

"There haven't been kids around here for the longest time," Aggie said. "I just love kids," she added.

Willow slumped down a littler farther and pretended like she didn't see her father motioning for her to get out of the truck.

She didn't want to get out of the truck.

She wanted to go home.

Back to the little brick house with the screened porch.

Her father motioned again and said, "Please come here, Willow," in that voice Willow hated.

So Willow got out of the truck and stood beside her father, looking down at her pink plastic sandals.

"I figured we should make arrangements for the inspection," Willow's father said to Aggie. "And get the rest of the paperwork done and all."

Aggie's hand fluttered up to her glasses, smoothed her hair, pushed at the sleeve of her sweater. "Um, well, okay." The corners of her mouth twitched. "But there's no hurry, right? I mean, you wanna be sure and all, and I . . ."

Willow studied Aggie's face. She couldn't put a name to what she saw there, but she knew that Aggie didn't want to sell this motel.

She looked around her at the ramshackle place and wondered why.

Why would anyone want to keep an awful old place like this?

Kirby explored every inch of the room while his mother took a nap.

The lamps with little black bears on the shades. The bedspread printed with cowboys and Indians, covered wagons and tepees. The tiny bathroom that smelled like mildew. The Bible on the bedside table.

He opened and closed all the drawers in the dresser. There was a book of matches way in the back of one. Kirby examined it. *Mountaintop Steakhouse* was printed on the front. Kirby put the matches in his pocket and went outside.

A red pickup truck was parked out front. That old lady, Aggie, was talking to a tall man with buzz-cut hair. Part of a tattoo peeked out from under the sleeve of his shirt. Beside him was a blond-haired girl, shuffling around in the gravel with the toe of her pink sandal.

Kirby went out to the swimming pool and bounced on the diving board. Then he walked around the edge. Heel to toe. Heel to toe. He kicked gravel into the empty pool.

He glanced over at the girl and the man talking to Aggie. The girl was still tracing circles in the dirt with her shoe.

Kirby picked up a piece of gravel and hurled it at the motel sign. It hit dead center with an echoey *thwack*, then ricocheted clear across the parking lot, landing right at the girl's feet.

The girl jumped.

The old lady said, "Oh, my!"

The man glared over at him.

Kirby grinned.

⦿ ⦿ ⦿

He spent the rest of the afternoon wandering around the motel. He looked in the windows of all the rooms. He checked the coin return on the soda machine. He went around back and explored the weed-filled vegetable garden, the toolshed, the woods.

When he finally went back to Room 1, his mother was sitting on the side of the bed yelling into the telephone.

"I *need* that money, Virgil."

She slammed the receiver down.

Bam!

"There's tomatoes and cantaloupes and stuff in a garden out there," Kirby said, motioning toward the back of the motel.

His mother looked up at him. There were black smudges of mascara under her eyes. Her hair stood out from her head in tangled, frizzy puffs.

She got up and padded to the bathroom in her bare feet and shut the door. Kirby took her purse from the top of the dresser and peered inside. Way at the bottom was a crumpled dollar bill. He put it in his shirt pocket, tossed the purse back on the dresser, and went outside again.

"There's one!" Loretta hollered, pointing out the window of the van.

Her father turned into the gravel parking lot. The tiny motel looked old and run-down, but Loretta liked the name of it.

Sleepy Time.

A black cat slept in a chair by the office door. A red pickup truck was parked in front of one of the rooms.

"Perfect," her mother said. "I like the feel of this place." She climbed out of the van with a grunt. "I'll go find out if we can get a room," she said.

Loretta watched her mother disappear inside the motel

office. A redheaded boy walked barefoot from the empty swimming pool. Loretta waved at him, but he kept his head down, his thick hair falling over his eyes. He went into one of the rooms and closed the door behind him. Loretta saw him pull the curtain aside and peek out the window at them.

Loretta's mother came out of the office and called, "Park over there, Marvin."

Her father parked the van in front of Room 6 and Loretta jumped out. An old lady unlocked the door and motioned for them to follow her inside. Her thin cotton pants were rolled up at the bottom and held with safety pins.

"I hope y'all like this room," she said.

"*Like* it?" Loretta's mother said. "Why, it's just adorable. Look at that, Lulu." She pointed to a clear plastic bird feeder stuck on the outside of one of the windows. A tiny bird scratched around at a few seeds in the bottom.

"I keep forgetting to fill that one," the lady said. "But then, I reckon I shouldn't tempt Ugly too much, anyway, you know?" She winked at Loretta.

"Who's Ugly?" Loretta said.

"My cat."

"That black one out yonder?"

The lady nodded. "That ugly one."

"I think he's cute," Loretta said.

The lady chuckled. "Well, he's been around the block a few times, I can tell you that."

Loretta's father came in carrying their suitcases.

"My name's Aggie," the lady said.

Loretta's father tipped his hat and said, "Marvin."

He put his arm around his wife and said, "This is Irene."

Then he put his big, warm hand on top of Loretta's head and said, "And this here is Loretta."

Aggie showed them how to pull the sofa out to make a bed for Loretta. She took some little packs of soap out of her pocket and put them in the bathroom. Then she nodded toward the wall behind the bed.

"The office is right next door," she said. "Y'all holler if you need anything." She pointed to one ear with a crooked finger. "And I do mean holler," she added. "These old ears of mine ain't what they used to be."

☺ ☺ ☺

Loretta loved the little motel room.

She loved the flowered bedspread.

She loved the pine-paneled walls.

She loved the map of the Great Smoky Mountains National Park taped on the closet door.

She even loved the musty smell and the window with the

screen falling out and the light fixture that made a little buzzing sound.

She wondered if her other mother had stayed here and if she had loved it, too.

While her mother unpacked their things and her father cleaned out the cooler, Loretta put the box with all her other mother's earthly possessions on the little table beside the bed.

Then she went outside to look for Ugly.

Willow hated the little motel room. It smelled bad. The carpet was stained and dirty. The faucet in the bathroom dripped.

Plunk. Plunk. Plunk.

Her father said he would sleep on the lumpy pullout couch, but the bed didn't look much better.

Willow stared glumly out the window while her father studied all those papers from the bank.

Those papers he needed to buy the motel from Aggie.

"Daddy," Willow said.

Her father looked up from his paperwork.

"How will Mama know where we are?" Willow said.

"She'll know."

"But how?"

"I'll tell her."

"When?"

"Soon."

"Can she come stay here, too?" Willow said.

"Willow . . ." Her father took his glasses off. "Your mother has chosen to leave us."

"But where is she?"

"I've told you before. She's with her sister in Savannah." He put his glasses on and went back to his paperwork. "If she wants to contact us," he added, "she knows where your grandmother is."

Willow felt a blanket of sadness settle over her, weighing her down.

She went outside and sat in a rocking chair made out of tree branches. She buried her face in her knees and squeezed her eyes shut. Tight.

Then she whispered, "Dorothy, Dorothy, Dorothy," over and over again.

Loretta

That night, Loretta sat in the lawn chair outside the door to Room 6. Lightning bugs were beginning to flicker out across the parking lot.

She had finally coaxed Ugly to sleep on her lap. The red-headed boy came out and ambled around the motel, kicking rocks and glancing over at her every now and then. Down at the other end of the motel, a girl sat in a rocking chair, pushing against the pavement with her bare foot, making the chair rock.

Back and forth.

Back and forth.

Loretta called out "Hey," but the girl didn't look up.

"Come see this cat," Loretta called.

The girl looked up.

"Come see this cat," Loretta called again.

The girl stopped rocking. She got up and walked toward Loretta, her bare feet making soft, slapping noises on the pavement.

"Isn't he cute?" Loretta said, stroking Ugly's patchy fur.

The girl nodded.

"His name is Ugly," Loretta said.

She wiggled her arm, making the charm bracelet jingle. "My name's Loretta," she said. "What's yours?"

The girl looked down at her feet and said, "Willow."

Loretta jiggled her bracelet again. "I'm going into fifth grade," she said. "What grade are you going into?"

"Fourth."

Loretta scratched Ugly behind his chewed-up ear. "Fourth grade's easy," she said.

Ugly jumped off her lap and strolled up the walk toward the office.

Loretta asked Willow a lot of questions. Before long, she knew all about Willow.

She knew that Willow had a collection of china horses.

She knew that Willow used to live in a brick house with a screened porch and a swing set.

She knew that Willow's father was buying the Sleepy Time Motel.

And she knew that Willow's mother's name was Dorothy,

but Dorothy wasn't here. When Loretta asked where she was, Willow just shrugged.

Willow didn't ask Loretta any questions, so Loretta volunteered stuff. That she lived in Calhoun, Tennessee, and had bunk beds that had once belonged to her cousin Audrey, who had run away to get married. That she was going to take karate lessons in the fall. That she stepped on a rusty nail when she was eight and had to get a tetanus shot.

Then she told Willow about the day she got the box of things that had belonged to her other mother.

She showed Willow all the charms on the bracelet and promised to show her the other things tomorrow.

Willow looked so sad, Loretta wondered if maybe Dorothy was dead.

"Is Dorothy dead?" she asked.

Willow shook her head.

Loretta could take a hint. She didn't ask any more questions about Dorothy.

"Come on, Ugly," Aggie said. "Let's go sit and ponder."

She sat in Harold's lounge chair and let Ugly curl up on the afghan in her lap. She looked out the window at the darkening sky.

"Maybe things are starting to change," she said. "I mean, *three* rooms in one day!"

She looked down at Ugly. "Maybe now I can fix things up," she said. "You know, the leaks in the roof and the clogged drains and all."

Ugly twitched one ear and purred up at her.

"Shoot, maybe I could even put water in that ole swimming pool again," she said. "Everyone always loved that pool. Remember, Ugly?"

Aggie closed her eyes and pictured the little swimming pool filled with sparkling blue water. Kids did cannonballs off the diving board, splashing their mothers sunning in the lounge chairs.

Thinking about the swimming pool reminded Aggie of the time the insurance man had come to the motel and made her and Harold put up that sign.

NO LIFEGUARD ON DUTY
SWIM AT YOUR OWN RISK

Aggie chuckled, thinking about how irritated Harold had gotten, telling that insurance man he was making a mountain out of a molehill.

Aggie's eyes popped open. Insurance? Had she paid that insurance bill? Where *was* that bill, anyway? Was it in the junk drawer with the other bills?

Aggie took a deep breath and let it out in a sigh that made Ugly jump off her lap and trot over to the kitchen to eat.

☺ ☺ ☺

Aggie slept in the lounge chair all night with the afghan pulled up to her chin. She didn't even wake up when the sun poured in through the window the next morning. She woke up when Clyde Dover banged on her door and called her name.

Aggie jumped.

"Coming," she answered, smoothing her hair and straightening her shirt.

When she opened the door she could hardly believe the sun was up so high and the day had begun.

"I can't hardly believe I slept this late," she said, opening the screen door for Mr. Dover.

"I'm sorry to bother you," he said, "but I thought maybe we could go over some things today."

"Things?"

"Um, yeah, you know, make a list of things."

Aggie cocked her head. "A list of things?"

Mr. Dover ran his hand over his buzz-cut hair. "Well, uh, yeah," he said. "Things we need to talk about before we sign the final papers."

Aggie stared at him. What kind of things was he talking about?

As if he'd read her mind, he said, "Um, like, things that need to be repaired and outstanding debts and all."

"Oh."

"And the inspector is coming this afternoon," he said. "If that's all right."

Aggie felt dizzy. She clutched the doorframe.

"Are you okay?" Mr. Dover asked.

Aggie said, "Yes," but she didn't feel okay. Dizzy, she could handle. Lord knows she'd been dizzy before.

But all this other stuff?

Final papers?

Inspector?

That stuff was harder to handle than a little ole dizzy spell.

Mr. Dover said something else, and Aggie nodded like she'd heard him (even though she hadn't), and then he left.

She washed her face and went outside to water her plants.

"What ya doin'?" someone called.

Aggie looked up to see Loretta, that little girl from Room 6, skipping toward her.

Aggie smiled.

She had forgotten all about skipping. How that felt, so happy and free.

When was the last time she had skipped? she wondered.

A long, long time ago, that was for sure.

"Just giving my pals some breakfast," she said.

Loretta examined the begonias and geraniums and marigolds in the mildewed flowerpots and rusty coffee cans outside the office door.

"But not really breakfast, right?" she said.

"Sure," Aggie said.

"Just water?"

Aggie snapped a yellow leaf off one of the begonias and tossed it into the gravel. "They hate Cheerios," she said.

Loretta giggled. A sparkly kind of giggle that made Aggie feel better about the day.

Loretta took a crumpled piece of paper out of the pocket of her shorts and showed it to Aggie.

"We're going to all these places," she said.

She beamed at Aggie and flicked her dark, straight hair out of her eyes with a dramatic shake of her head.

Aggie adjusted her glasses and squinted down at the paper. "Oh, my," she said. "That's a lot of places."

"I know." Then Loretta told Aggie all about her other mother and the charm bracelet. She held her arm up so Aggie could see all the charms.

Aggie examined every little silver charm and made sure she said something nice about each one.

"Lawd, look at that itty bitty little starfish!

"Well, I'll be darned. The Statue of Liberty! Ain't that something!"

Someone slammed a door.

Hard.

Kirby Tanner marched across the parking lot toward the road.

"Oh, Kirby," Aggie called.

Kirby glanced over his shoulder but kept on walking.

"Come meet Loretta."

Kirby stopped.

"Come see what she's got," Aggie said.

Kirby turned and walked back toward them, his hands shoved deep into his pockets and his shoulders hunched up around his ears.

Loretta jiggled her hand, making the charm bracelet jingle.

"Kirby, this is Loretta," Aggie said.

Kirby shifted from one foot to the other. Traced circles in the dirt with the toe of his sneaker. Cracked his knuckles. Smoothed his hair.

Loretta jabbered away about all the places she was going to visit in the Smoky Mountains.

And then Willow came out of her room and sat in the rocking chair.

"Willow," Aggie called over to her.

Willow looked up. Her blond hair looked almost white in the morning sun, framing her face with a halo of curls.

"Come here." Aggie motioned for Willow to join them.

Willow walked slowly toward them in a tiptoe kind of way, in her pink plastic sandals. Aggie felt a little stab at the sight of such a sad-looking girl.

Aggie wanted to hug her, but maybe Willow wouldn't want to be hugged.

So instead of hugging, Aggie said, "I love those sandals."

That afternoon, Willow sat outside Room 10, eating sliced cheese on saltine crackers and watching the man inspecting the motel. He poked at the rotting wood under the windows with a screwdriver. He scraped at the rust on the hot water tank. He examined the frayed electrical wires above the office door. And he scribbled things onto the papers on his clipboard.

Willow's father followed the inspector around like a stray dog. Pointing at things. Asking questions. Studying the clipboard.

When Willow got tired of watching them, she walked up and down the sidewalk out front, stepping carefully over the cracks. At one end of the motel, a path led around back. Willow followed it. Pricker bushes snagged her shorts and scratched her arms. As she neared the back of the motel, she thought she heard someone talking.

She stopped.

Yes, someone *was* talking.

Then someone laughed.

Then talking again.

She peered around the corner. Aggie stood in the middle of a dried-up, overgrown garden. A plastic milk carton with the top cut off hung from a string around her neck. When Aggie looked up, Willow ducked back around the corner of the motel.

"Is that you, Willow?" Aggie called out.

Willow stepped around the corner and waved at Aggie. A small, floppy-handed wave.

"The rabbits are getting all my pole beans," Aggie said. She shook the milk carton. "Six," she said. "Six measly ole beans."

"Oh," Willow said.

"Good thing I don't eat much." Aggie stooped to pull a half-eaten cantaloupe out of the yellowing vines. "Looks like them dern rabbits had dessert, too."

Willow stepped over a twisted clump of kudzu meandering across the path. She looked around her at the dried-up tangle of a garden.

"I thought I heard someone talking back here," she said to Aggie.

Aggie raised her eyebrows. "Back here?" She swatted at a cloud of gnats hovering in front of her face. "Naw." She shook her head. "Ain't nobody back here but me and Harold."

"Harold?"

"Well, not *Harold* Harold," Aggie said. "But, you know"— she pointed at the sky with a crooked finger—"Harold."

Willow looked up at the puffy white clouds.

"Harold?" she said again.

Aggie nodded. "He keeled right over in the tomato garden." She gestured toward a cluster of droopy tomato plants inside a square of picket fence. They spilled out of bent-up wire cages, sagging under the weight of rotting tomatoes.

Willow shivered, thinking about a dead man in there.

"I come out here to ask his opinion every now and then," Aggie said.

"Oh." Willow wondered if maybe Aggie was crazy. She studied the old woman's wrinkled face, her wispy gray hair, her sparkly blue eyes. She didn't really *look* like a crazy person, but still . . .

"Is that nosy clipboard man gone yet?" Aggie said.

Willow shook her head.

Aggie took a bean out of the milk carton and snapped it

in two. She popped half in her mouth and handed the other half to Willow.

Willow had never eaten a raw bean before. It was warm and kind of fuzzy.

Aggie brushed leaves off a dirty plastic chair beside the garden and sat down with a sigh. Willow sat beside her on an overturned milk crate. She wondered if Harold had sat on that crate.

They sat like that for a while.

Not talking.

Watching the dragonflies flit around the garden.

Listening to the grasshoppers buzzing in the weeds.

And then Aggie told Willow all about Harold. How he could do magic tricks with paper cups and how he made up songs about things, like garbage and snakes and chewing gum.

She told her about the day she and Harold had opened the Sleepy Time Motel, way back when it was brand-new and a steady stream of tourists snaked up the mountain roads in the summertime.

"I still have the guest book signed by the very first folks who ever stayed here," Aggie said. "Carl and Libby Elfers from Chapel Hill, North Carolina."

While Aggie told Willow about how she and Harold had worked from sunup to sundown washing towels and changing lightbulbs and refilling the soda machine, her eyes twinkled and danced like she was seeing Harold right there in front of her.

But then her face drooped when she told Willow about how the interstate highway was built and the tourists zoomed up to the mountaintop without ever laying eyes on the Sleepy Time Motel.

And then things had slowed down a little.

And then things had slowed down a lot.

"And then, well, things just kind of got away from us," Aggie said.

And now Harold was gone.

And then Aggie stopped talking.

Willow looked down at Aggie's canvas sneakers. They were wet and muddy. One of them had a frayed hole in the side and Aggie's little toe poked out.

Willow reached into her shirt pocket and pulled out a tiny china horse. The trotting white one that her friend Maggie had given her for her birthday last year. She held it out toward Aggie in the palm of her hand.

"If you keep this for a while, it will bring you good luck," she said.

Aggie took the little horse and examined it. Then she put it in the plastic milk carton on top of the beans.

"Thank you," she said.

She put her wrinkled, brown-spotted hand on Willow's knee.

"Wanna help me finish watering the begonias?" she said.

Willow nodded. "Okay."

As they made their way along the overgrown path out of the garden, Willow decided that maybe Aggie wasn't crazy, after all.

Kirby sat beside the swimming pool and opened the shoebox from Burla. Tucked inside was a lumpy foil package. Kirby pulled back the foil. Cookies. The kind with a dab of strawberry jam in the scooped-out middle. Thumbprint cookies, Burla called them.

Under the foil package were three sheets of paper, three envelopes, and three stamps.

A ballpoint pen from Southside Baptist Church.

Some bubble gum.

A purple yo-yo.

And a picture of Burla's dog, Barney, sitting on Burla's quilt-covered couch with his tongue hanging out and a doggy grin on his face. He looked a lot younger than he was now.

His face wasn't gray.

His eyes weren't cloudy.

His teeth weren't yellow.

Kirby felt a pang in his heart for Barney.

Kirby took a cookie out of the foil package and licked the strawberry jam out of the middle. Then he put his thumb in the scooped-out part. The part where Burla's thumb had been.

He took the folded postcard out of his pocket. *Greetings from the Great Smoky Mountains*. He tossed it into the box with the other things. Then he walked around the edge of the pool, thinking about what a mess he was in.

Kicked out of school for no good reason.

Hollered at all the time by his hateful old stepfather, Virgil.

Treated like dirt by his very own father.

The only time his mother paid any attention to him at all was when he got in trouble. Most times it was *Ace this* and *Ace that.*

Ace, his perfect brother.

Kirby had figured out a long time ago that the only thing he could do better than Ace was get in trouble.

So that's what he did.

Now he was being hauled off to some awful school where they made you do chores and push-ups and say *yes, sir* and *no, sir.*

The crunch of tires on gravel interrupted Kirby's thoughts. That red pickup truck. Mr. Dover jumped out, whistling. He waved at Kirby, then helped Aggie down from the other side of the truck. The two of them disappeared inside the office.

Kirby took a piece of paper and the pen out of the box and sat on the concrete steps of the swimming pool to write.

Dear Burla,
   How are you? I am fine.

He chewed on the end of the pen and looked up at the sky. Then in front of the word *fine*, he squeezed in the word *NOT.*

I am NOT fine.

Then he made a list of all the reasons he was not fine. Number one was that bad-boy school waiting for him up the winding mountain road. Number seven was being stuck in this falling-apart motel. And in between was his mama acting so mean and their broken-down car and a girl named Willow with stupid plastic sandals and another girl named Loretta who talked all the time and jingled a bracelet every minute of the day. And a skinny old woman named Aggie. (But then he scratched out the word *old* because Burla was old, too, so maybe she wouldn't like it if he said that.)

Then he wrote two things that *were* fine: a cat named Ugly who liked him a lot and the thumbprint cookies.

The screen door of the office banged and Kirby looked up. Aggie sat in the lawn chair out front. Willow came out and sat beside her. Kirby looked down real quick, thinking that any minute Aggie was going to call to him. Wave her bony old hand and motion for him to come over there. Make him talk to her and Willow.

But she didn't.

Kirby looked over at them again. Aggie sat all hunched over and droopy-looking. Willow looked down at her hands, clasped in her lap. She crossed her ankles and swung her legs. Back and forth. Back and forth.

Tires on gravel again. The white van with *Murphy's Heating and Plumbing* on the side. That girl Loretta and her parents. All of them smiling and waving and acting like the Sleepy Time Motel was Disney World or something.

Loretta jumped out and ran over to him.

"Guess where we've been," she said.

Kirby shrugged.

"Dollywood!" Loretta practically hollered.

Kirby said, "So?" but Loretta must have thought he said, "Tell me all about it," because she went on and on about all the stuff at Dollywood.

"It's over in Pigeon Forge," she said. "There's all these rides there. One's called the Thunderhead and it's really scary. And the Dizzy Disk made us kinda sick. And I went on the Shooting Star all by myself." She sat on the steps beside Kirby. "And I tried on one of Dolly Parton's very own wigs," she said. "From her Chasing Rainbows museum that has all her outfits and things."

"How come?" Kirby asked.

"How come what?"

"How come you tried on her wigs?"

Loretta's eyebrows squeezed together. " *'Cause,*" she said real drawn out and whiny-like. "I mean, *Dolly Parton*?"

Loretta jingled her charm bracelet. "And guess what else?" she said.

Kirby swatted at a fly and waited.

"I got a charm for my bracelet," Loretta said. "A little heart that opens up and has *Dollywood* on the inside."

Kirby swatted the fly again. "So?"

Loretta nodded toward the shoebox in Kirby's lap. "What's that?" she said.

"Stuff."

"What kind of stuff?"

Kirby put his arm over the top of the box. This crazy girl was liable to snatch it away from him or something.

"Just stuff," he said.

"I have a box of stuff, too," Loretta said. "From my other mother who died."

Kirby sat up straight.

Other mother who died?

And then Loretta went skipping off across the parking lot, calling over her shoulder, "Come on, I'll show you."

Loretta

"And look at these." Loretta held out the silver scissors shaped like a bird so Kirby could see.

"And that." Loretta pointed to the Japanese fan.

Kirby picked the fan up and opened and closed it until Loretta took it away from him.

He examined the pocket watch. He thumbed through the white leather Bible. He picked up the sparkly poodle dog pin. He turned it over and studied the back. He ran his finger over the shiny green stones that were the poodle eyes.

"Emeralds," Loretta said, pointing at the shiny little eyes.

"These ain't real emeralds," he said.

Loretta snatched the pin from him.

"How come you have two mothers?" Kirby said. "And what happened to the other one?"

So Loretta told him how she had been adopted by Irene and Marvin Murphy when she was a tiny baby. Then she told him about the box of earthly possessions that came in the mail and the note about her other mother passing on to the other side.

She jingled the charm bracelet in his face and pointed out each of the charms.

"We're going to visit all the places my other mother visited," she said. "And look at this." She smoothed the blue handkerchief out on the bed and pointed to the letter *P* embroidered in the corner with shiny pink thread. "I was thinking the *P* probably stands for Pamela. Or maybe just Pam."

"You don't even know her name?" Kirby said.

"No, but I bet it was Pam."

Loretta jammed everything back in the box, clamped the lid on, and said, "Let's go find Willow."

◉ ◉ ◉

"But why would she sell the motel if she doesn't want to?" Loretta asked Willow.

"Because she can't take care of it by herself," Willow said. "Without Harold," she added.

Loretta sat next to Willow in the damp grass surrounding the flagpole. Kirby hopped around them, counting.

Twenty hops on the right foot.

Twenty hops on the left foot.

The sun had begun to sink below the mountains and stars twinkled dimly in the clear sky.

"So why doesn't she hire somebody to help?" Loretta said. "Like a handyman or something."

"Because she doesn't have any money." Willow picked at blades of grass. "Because nobody comes here anymore. Everybody wants to stay at those fancy places down on the interstate."

Loretta tucked a strand of hair behind her ear. "Then why does your dad want to buy this motel anyways?"

Willow's face crumpled up in a heap of wailing tears and she ran off to her room in her tippy-toe way, her plastic sandals making squeaky noises on the sidewalk.

Loretta looked at Kirby.

Kirby shrugged.

Loretta glanced over at the swimming pool. Her mother was sitting in a lounge chair talking to Mr. Dover. Her father was fiddling with wires hanging out of the floodlight beside the Sleepy Time Motel sign, his tools spread out in the weeds beside his toolbox.

There was a buzzing sound and then a popping sound and then another buzzing sound and suddenly the Sleepy

Time Motel sign was shining bright as anything in the glow of the floodlight.

Loretta's mother clapped and Mr. Dover whooped.

Loretta looked over at the office. Aggie was peering out from behind the curtain.

"Let's go talk to Aggie," Loretta said to Kirby.

But before they got to the office door, Kirby's mother came storming across the parking lot from the road.

"Get on inside," she hollered at Kirby.

Kirby's shoulders slumped and he mumbled, "Bye."

Loretta watched him follow his mother up the sidewalk to their room and disappear inside.

Then she ran on over to the office to talk to Aggie.

Aggie put a red X through the day on the calendar. A bad day, she thought.

Everything had happened so fast. Clyde Dover had only arrived yesterday. Why was he in such an all-fired hurry—making lists and yakking with that inspector and driving her down to the bank to sign more papers? Why couldn't they just slow down a little bit?

Signing her name on all those papers over at the bank had made her head hurt and her stomach queasy.

Agnes Duncan.

Agnes Duncan.

Agnes Duncan.

Over and over again.

Each time feeling worse than the time before.

And then Agnes Duncan on the very last page and the Sleepy Time Motel wasn't hers anymore.

Aggie shuffled around the office in her bedroom slippers. She tidied up the postcards and straightened the stack of maps and then she noticed something. Down at one end of the counter. A pair of sunglasses. Some pens. A yellow folder with *Motel* scrawled on the front with a black marker.

Clyde Dover's folder.

Aggie switched on the lamp with a shaky hand. A jacket hung on a peg behind the counter. A denim jacket that wasn't hers and wasn't Harold's.

Clyde Dover's denim jacket.

"Well, now . . ." she said.

She pulled back the dusty curtains and peered outside. The Sleepy Time Motel sign glowed in the darkening sky.

"Well, now . . ." she said again.

She went outside to sweep the sidewalk in front of the office.

"Hey, Aggie."

Aggie looked up to see Loretta running toward her.

"Willow said you sold the motel," Loretta said. "How come?"

Aggie dropped into the lawn chair by the door. "It's a long story and a short day," she said.

"Oh." Loretta sat beside her, swinging her legs, slapping her bare feet against the sidewalk.

Aggie took a deep breath of the cool night air. She watched the lights flick on down in Kirby's room. She admired the glow of the Sleepy Time Motel sign. Then she sat back and listened while Loretta told her all about Dollywood. About the rides and the wigs and all. Every now and then, she reached into her pocket to feel the little china horse that Willow had given her.

"And I bet my other mother tried on a wig, too, don't you?" Loretta said.

Aggie nodded. "Most definitely," she said.

"Her name was Pam."

"Really?"

"Well, maybe . . ." Loretta clapped her hands at a mosquito that flitted around in front of them. "Or Patsy," she said. "Maybe Patsy."

Aggie was glad to have Loretta sitting there next to her, swinging her legs and jangling her bracelet and chattering on and on about her other mother in that happy way of hers.

And so it seemed like that bad day was going to end as a good one.

Or at least a not-so-bad one.

But then Clyde Dover came over and asked Aggie for a key to the office.

A key for him.

A key so he could lock up, since, you know, his stuff was in there now.

And the whole time Aggie was looking for that spare key that she knew was in the junk drawer somewhere, he was rambling on and on about all the things he was going to change. Paint the office. Move the soda machine. Maybe even pave the parking lot.

"And there's something else I've got in mind," he said, "but it's a surprise."

Aggie's not-so-bad day was turning back into a bad day.

That night, she slept sitting up in Harold's old lounge chair again, clutching the little china horse and dreaming about Dolly Parton.

Willow's life wasn't almost perfect anymore.

It wasn't even close to perfect.

In fact, it was far, far from perfect.

Her worries were piling up, one on top of the other, like bricks on a wall.

First, her father had bought a new life and their old life was history. They weren't going back to their little brick house in Hailey ever again.

Willow's next worry was Dorothy.

Dorothy was with her sister down in Savannah, Georgia.

Savannah, Georgia, was a long way from Shawnee Gap, North Carolina.

And then there was Aggie.

The Sleepy Time Motel had belonged to Aggie and Harold. The ten little rooms. The sign and the swimming pool. The bird feeders, the flagpole, the garden.

All of those things had been theirs.

But now Harold was gone and Willow's father had "closed the deal," so all that stuff belonged to him. Willow could see happiness all over her father and sadness all over Aggie.

Something about that seemed just plain wrong to Willow.

And now here she was, sitting on a stool behind the counter in the motel office, waiting for guests to come and check in. That would be her job, checking the guests in. At least until school started in a few weeks, her father had said. She would ask the guests to sign the big leather guest book. Give them a map. Sell them some postcards. Give them a room key.

The screen door squeaked open and Kirby stepped in. He looked surprised when he saw Willow.

"Oh, hey," he said.

"Hey."

"My mom told me to see if we got any mail." Kirby shifted from one foot to the other. He cracked his knuckles. He popped his bubble gum. He pushed his greasy red hair out of his eyes.

"I'll check," Willow said.

She pulled a cardboard box out from under the counter and looked through the pile of mail.

Kirby paced around the room, touching things, moving things. He gave the postcard rack a spin.

Willow pushed the cardboard box back up under the counter. "No mail," she said.

"Okay." Kirby darted out the door, letting it bang shut behind him.

Willow went out on the sidewalk and watched Kirby running in a zigzag path back to his room. A few minutes later, he came out again, with that shoebox of his tucked under his arm. He ran over to the swimming pool and sat on the diving board. Then he took a pen and paper out of the box and began to write.

Willow went back inside and sat on the stool behind the counter again. She wished Aggie would come out of her room and talk to her. She wished Loretta weren't packing for a picnic over in Maggie Valley. She wished Dorothy would leave Savannah and come be with her. She wished she could go back to one of those days on the kitchen calendar that had Dorothy's loopy handwriting on it.

Willow's school play.

That would be a good day to go back to. Willow would be on the stage dressed like Betsy Ross, sewing a flag, and Dorothy would be sitting out there in the auditorium smiling up at her.

But none of those wishes came true.

Instead, Willow's father came into the office and said, "Those sign guys are coming tomorrow afternoon."

"What sign guys?"

"The guys who are bringing the new sign."

"What new sign?"

Willow's father ran his hand over his hair. "Well, the new motel sign."

"What's wrong with the old sign?" Willow said.

Her father fiddled with papers on the counter. "Well, actually," he said, "I was thinking we'd spruce things up a bit, you know?"

Her father moved the stack of maps from one end of the counter to the other. "This place looks, too, well, you know, old-fashioned," he said. "If we're going to attract tourists we've got to—"

"I think the sign looks nice," Willow said. She glanced back at the curtain over the doorway to Aggie's room.

Her father went on and on about all the plans he had for the motel.

The new sign.

The color of the paint in Room 3.

The king-sized bed in Room 8.

The ad in the newspaper.

The billboard down by the main highway.

But Willow wasn't really paying attention. She was thinking maybe she'd give Aggie another china horse.

"No, Virgil, the money did *not* get here."

Kirby watched the back of his mother's head as she talked on the phone. Ringlets of damp hair stuck to her neck.

"I've been living on bread and peanut butter for three days, Virgil!" she hollered. "I feel like just taking the bus home and leaving that junk heap by the side of the road."

"What about me?" Kirby whispered.

His mother slammed the receiver down. She rubbed her temples in little circles.

Kirby traced a tepee on the bedspread with his finger. He glanced over at his duffel bag by the door.

"So, I guess we ain't leaving for a while, right?" he said.

His mother flopped back on the bed and put her arm over her face.

"I got no money. I got no car," she said.

Kirby smiled.

"Good," he whispered.

His mother shot up and glared at him.

"What'd you say?" she snapped.

"Nothing." Kirby traced a galloping horse on the bedspread.

His mother flopped back down on the bed and Kirby went outside. A soft, misty rain had begun falling, already leaving little puddles scattered over the muddy gravel parking lot. Kirby jumped from puddle to puddle, swinging the purple yo-yo Burla had given him over his head like a lasso.

"That's dangerous."

Kirby looked over at Loretta, sitting in her bathing suit at the picnic table out by the flagpole. She was putting the box of things from her other mother into a plastic grocery bag on her lap.

Kirby swung the yo-yo harder. It made a buzzing sound as it whipped through the air.

"We can't go to Maggie Valley 'cause of the rain," Loretta said.

Kirby swung the yo-yo harder, sending drops of rain flying in every direction.

"O-say at-whay," he said.

"What?" Loretta said, jiggling that bracelet of hers on her skinny arm.

"Othing-nay."

"Did your car get fixed?" Loretta said.

"Ope-nay."

Kirby did a few of those yo-yo tricks his Uncle Lester had taught him.

Around the Corner.

The Creeper.

Dizzy Baby.

"Show me how to do that," Loretta said.

"Naw."

Loretta put her hands together like she was praying. "Please," she said.

Kirby put the yo-yo in the pocket of his shorts.

"Maybe later," he said.

Loretta squeezed her lips together and glared at him. Then she jumped off the picnic table and stormed off with her box tucked under her arm.

Kirby hopped over a puddle, landing in the mud with a splat. He picked up a stick and hurled it clear across the parking lot and into the ditch on the other side of the road. He practiced a few more yo-yo tricks.

Runaway Dog.

Drop in the Bucket.

He put the yo-yo back in his pocket and jumped over puddles in big, giant leaps, counting out loud.

One. Two. Three.

When he got to the swimming pool, he hopped down the cement steps on one foot and back up them on the other. He bounced on the diving board.

And then he stopped.

What was that?

Something shiny out there in the grass by the flagpole.

He ran over to see what it was.

A sparkly poodle dog pin with shiny green eyes.

Loretta's pin.

Kirby wiped the mud off it with his shirttail and put it in his pocket with the yo-yo.

Loretta studied the silver pocket watch.

"W, K, L," she whispered, tracing the letters engraved on the back.

Her father had said the watch probably once belonged to a man. Loretta had thought and thought about who the man could have been. Her other mother's father? Her uncle? Maybe her grandfather?

"Mama?" Loretta said.

Her mother looked up from her crossword puzzle and said, "Hmmm?"

"I bet this watch belonged to her father," Loretta said.

Her mother nodded. "You could be right, Lulu," she said.

"And so that means her last name started with an *L*." Loretta pointed to the *L* on the back of the pocket watch.

Her mother adjusted her glasses and studied the watch. "Could be," she said.

"Pam Lawrence," Loretta said. "Maybe *that* was her name."

Her mother smiled. "Maybe," she said.

Loretta put the watch back in the box. She looked at the hummingbird picture. She rubbed the soft leather cover of the Bible.

Suddenly she jumped up and dumped everything out of the box onto the bed. Frantically, she searched through the things.

"Mama!" she hollered. "Something's missing!"

Her mother set her crossword puzzle aside. "What's missing?" she said.

"I don't know," Loretta said. "Something . . ."

Loretta tapped each thing on the bed. The fan. The scissors. The heart-shaped box.

"The dog!" she said. "The poodle dog pin."

Loretta dropped to her knees and searched the floor, patting the thick green carpet. Under the bed. Under the dresser. Beside the desk.

Her mother looked in drawers. She emptied their suitcases. She searched the bathroom, all the while saying, "We'll find it, Lulu . . . Don't cry, Lulu."

But Loretta did cry. She ran around the little motel room, searching for the poodle dog pin and sobbing.

And then she remembered she had taken the box of stuff outside.

She dashed out of the room and looked everywhere for the sparkly pin. In the parking lot. Up and down the sidewalk. Under the picnic table. Out by the diving board.

Finally, she sat on the wet grass by the flagpole and put her head on her knees.

"What's wrong, Loretta?"

Loretta looked up. Aggie was bending over her. She was wearing a clear plastic rain hat tied under her chin with a red ribbon.

"I lost my other mother's poodle dog pin," Loretta said in a trembly voice.

"Oh, dear," Aggie said.

Loretta had never felt so miserable. Those things had been all of her other mother's earthly possessions and now one of them was gone.

And it was all her fault.

Why, why, why had she brought that box outside?

Loretta felt Aggie's warm hand on her shoulder.

"I hate losing things, too," Aggie said. "But you know what?"

"What?"

"I have a real knack for finding lost things."

"You do?"

Aggie nodded. "If I had a nickel for every time Harold lost his glasses, well, shoot, I'd be richer than the Queen of England. And don't you know it was me that found 'em every time."

"Really?"

"That's right." Aggie stroked Loretta's hair. "And one time some folks from way up in New York lost their car keys and like to gone crazy till I found 'em. And guess where they were."

"Where?

"In one of my flowerpots." Aggie chuckled. "Right down in there with the begonias."

Loretta stood up and brushed the wet grass from the backs of her legs.

"Aren't you smart wearing your bathing suit in this wet weather?" Aggie said.

Loretta looked down at her mud-splattered bathing suit and shrugged. She didn't tell Aggie that she had put on her bathing suit so she could pose in front of the mirror, pretending like she was on a rock in the middle of a creek, holding a towel—just like her other mother in that photo in the box.

"I'll help you look for that pin, okay?" Aggie said.

Loretta nodded, brushing strands of wet hair out of her eyes.

Loretta and Aggie looked for the poodle dog pin all afternoon. Under Clyde Dover's pickup truck. All around the sign out by the road. Even in Aggie's begonias.

Loretta's mother joined them, telling Loretta over and over not to worry. They would find it.

When Loretta's father finished helping Clyde Dover fix the clogged drain in Room 4, he joined them, too. Even Ugly ambled along beside them as they searched, stopping every now and then to lick the rain off his scruffy black coat.

But no one found the sparkly poodle dog pin.

Not even Aggie, who had always been so good at finding things.

Aggie hung her wet jacket on the hook behind the door and took off her muddy rubber boots.

"I can't believe I can't find that pin," she said to Ugly.

Aggie had been so certain she was going to find Loretta's pin. She had looked for hours yesterday and again first thing this morning.

But she hadn't found it.

"Maybe I've lost my touch," she said to Ugly.

She slipped into her ratty old bedroom slippers and put the kettle on the stove.

"We might as well have some tea before we, well, you know . . ." she said.

She couldn't bring herself to say the word out loud.

Pack.

Pack her things.

Pack Harold's things.

Pack all their things in boxes so Clayton Underwood could take them to her cousin Evelyn's place over in Raleigh.

While she sipped her tea, Aggie watched the rain outside. Every now and then she glanced over at the cardboard boxes by the door. Clayton Underwood had brought them when he'd delivered her groceries, and she had thanked him and promised she'd have them packed by next week so he could pick them up. She had written *Clothes* on one and *Kitchen* on one and *Other Stuff* on one.

But she didn't know where to start.

How do you pack a life? she wondered.

"Aggie?"

Aggie jumped.

"Aggie?"

Aggie recognized that soft little voice coming from the other side of the curtain over the office door.

"Is that you, Willow?" Aggie said.

Willow pulled the curtain aside and stood in the doorway, looking like the shyest child Aggie had ever seen in all her born days.

"Come in, sweetheart," Aggie said. "Me and Ugly are just sitting here having some tea."

"Oh."

"Would you like some?"

"No, ma'am."

"Nasty weather out there."

Willow glanced out the window and nodded. Then she stepped into the room.

"I brought you something," she said.

"You did?"

Willow held out her hand. A china horse. A galloping black stallion.

Aggie felt her worried face soften and her heavy heart lift, and all she could do was shake her head in amazement at how a little ole thing like a china horse could change things so much.

She set her teacup on the TV tray beside the chair and motioned for Willow to come over to her.

Willow walked with one foot in front of the other, ever so slowly, like she was balancing on a log. When she got to Harold's chair, Aggie hugged her.

She was surprised how small and fragile Willow was. Such a frail wisp of a girl.

And then Aggie felt Willow's arms around her neck, hugging her back.

"His name is Lightning," Willow said, looking down at the little horse in the palm of her hand. "You can keep him," she added.

Aggie took the horse from Willow and studied it.

"You know, my Uncle Nathan used to have a horse looked just like this," Aggie said.

"Really?"

"Sure did. Me and my cousin Evelyn used to ride him bareback. You ever ride bareback?"

Willow shook her head. "I never rode a horse at all," she said.

Aggie slapped her knee. "You don't mean that," she said.

"Yes, ma'am, I do."

"Well, I bet you've done plenty of things I've never done."

Willow shrugged.

Ugly leaped off the chair and strolled along the orange carpet path toward the door. Then he jumped inside one of the cardboard boxes.

"What are those?" Willow said, pointing.

"Oh, well, those are for, um, packing."

There, Aggie thought. She had said it.

"Packing?" Willow's eyebrows squeezed together.

"Clayton Underwood's gonna have a conniption fit if them boxes ain't ready by next week."

"Ready for what?" Willow said.

"Um, well, ready for him to take 'em over to my cousin Evelyn's place in Raleigh."

"How come?"

Aggie looked down at the china horse in her hand and was nearly knocked over by the smothering sadness that fell over the room. It swirled around her and it swirled around Willow. It seeped into every corner of the room, climbing over Harold's lounge chair and slithering along the tabletops and snaking through the begonias.

Finally Willow's voice broke the silence. "Why do you have to leave?" she said, sitting on the bed across from Aggie.

So Aggie explained to Willow that this room wasn't hers anymore. She told her about Evelyn's condominium over in Raleigh. How there was an extra bedroom with pink striped wallpaper that she had never seen but Evelyn had said was real nice. There was a laundry room with six washers and six dryers, a heated swimming pool, and a community room where folks could watch movies on Mondays and play cards on Wednesdays.

"And they allow cats," Aggie said, looking over at Ugly sitting in the box marked *Kitchen*. "Although Evelyn never has cared much for cats," she added.

"But don't you want to stay here?" Willow said, twisting a strand of her thin blond hair around and around her finger.

Aggie studied Willow's face. Her serious eyes. Her quivering chin. If there was ever a child who needed to hear the truth, the forlorn little girl sitting in front of her was it.

So Aggie said, "Yes. I do want to stay here."

"Then why don't you?" Willow said.

Aggie's hand fluttered up and adjusted her glasses. "Well, you know, life marches on. And sometimes we have to join the parade whether we want to or not." Aggie took both of Willow's hands in hers. "You know what I mean?" she said.

Willow lifted her thin shoulders and let them drop with a sigh. She drew her legs up and hugged her knees, looking for all the world like she intended to stay there forever.

Aggie waited.

And then Willow told her all about Dorothy.

How she used to make gingerbread every Friday.

How she had read the Bible cover to cover and once broke her arm trying to get a cat off the roof.

How she had named Willow after her favorite tree and sometimes wore her sweaters backwards just for fun.

How she believed that if you walk into a cobweb, you'll get a letter from someone you love.

How she and Willow's dad had just stopped loving each other and so she had left.

Then Willow got quiet and they all just sat there.

Willow on the bed.

Aggie in Harold's chair.

And Ugly in the *Kitchen* box.

The rain splattered against the windows and ran down the glass in wavy little rivers.

Aggie's thoughts were bouncing all around—from Willow to that condominium over in Raleigh to those boxes stacked up by the door and back to Willow again.

"I know your mama loves you a lot," she said.

Willow shrugged and picked at a thread on the button of her shirt. "I'm pretty sure she used to," she said so soft and low that Aggie had to lean forward to hear her.

Aggie slapped her hands on the arms of the chair so hard that Willow jumped. *"Used to?"* Aggie said. "Listen to you." She peered up into Willow's face. "I guaran-dern-tee you that as sure as the sun comes up in the morning, that mother of yours loves you to pieces."

"Then why'd she leave me?" Willow said.

"Just got in the wrong parade, I reckon."

Willow cocked her head like she was thinking it over.

Aggie pushed her glasses up on her nose. "What I mean is, she just veered off in a different direction from the one she was going in before." She patted Willow's knee. "She ain't forgot you, sweetheart."

Aggie studied Willow. Her curly blond hair swirling around her face. Her peeling pink fingernail polish. The spattering of pale freckles on her arms.

"Well, would you look at that?" Aggie pointed out the window. "The sun came out."

Willow looked out the window and nodded.

"Let's go say hey to Harold," Aggie said. "You know, back there in the garden."

"Okay."

Outside, the air smelled fresh and clean. Queen Anne's lace, heavy from the rain, bowed down along the roadside. A tiny wren splashed in a puddle of muddy water in the parking lot.

With Ugly strolling along beside them, Aggie and Willow walked around back to the garden, hand in hand, to say hello to Harold.

Willow had a stomachache.

She sat in the rocking chair in front of Room 10 and made a list inside her head of all the reasons she had a stomachache.

- *Dorothy*
- *Those cardboard boxes over in Aggie's room*
- *That boy Kirby, hopping all around out there in the parking lot*
- *Dorothy*
- *The new motel sign that was on its way here at this very minute*
- *Dorothy*

Willow was supposed to be inside, eating the ham sandwich her father had made for lunch.

But she had a stomachache.

She stayed out in the rocking chair and waited for Clayton Underwood to bring the mail.

Maybe he would bring a letter from Dorothy.

After a while, Willow got tired of waiting, so she went down to the office to watch her father paint.

"This will cheer the place up a bit," her father said, swiping bright yellow paint over the dingy gray wall.

"What about those?" Willow pointed to the cup hooks lying in a pile on the counter.

The cup hooks that used to be on the wall to hang the room keys on.

Her father glanced at them and shrugged. "I don't know. They seem kind of old-fashioned to me."

"Not to me."

"Anyway," her father went on, "I was thinking we should change all the locks on the doors and have those cards. You know, like fancy hotels have."

Willow shook her head. "That's a bad idea."

Her father kept painting. "And I'm thinking we should charge for those maps." He nodded toward the stack of maps on the counter. "Maybe a dollar?" He looked at Willow. "What do you think?"

"I think they should be free."

Her father tossed the paintbrush onto the newspaper on the floor and sighed.

"Willow," he said. "A lot of things around here need changing, and your attitude is one of 'em."

Willow kept her gaze on the counter in front of her. She swung one leg back and forth, hitting the stool with her heel.

Thunk. Thunk. Thunk.

Her father picked up the paintbrush again.

"If we're gonna make this place work, we've gotta *change* things," he said.

"Why?" Willow's voice was soft and trembly.

Her father let out another sigh.

A big, heaving sigh.

"You said yourself this place is awful," he said. "You hate the carpet and you hate the swimming pool and you—"

"Well, I don't anymore." Willow kept thunking the stool. "Why does Aggie have to leave?" she said.

And then her father did what he always did. He closed right up. He shut his mouth and he shut his mind and he shut his heart. Sealed it all up and threw away the key.

So Willow left the office and went around back to the garden. Raindrops still glistened on the droopy leaves of the beans and tomatoes and melons. She sat on the milk crate and wished she were back in the little brick house in Hailey, playing with Maggie, trotting her china horses around the screened porch until Dorothy called her in for dinner.

When Willow got tired of wishing, she headed back up the path out of the garden. And just as she was rounding the corner of the motel, she felt something on her face.

A cobweb.

The soft strands of a cobweb, stretching across her face and in her hair.

Kirby sat in the lawn chair outside his room and took out the shoebox that Burla had given him.

Dear Burla,

    How is Barney? I hope he is good.

    ~~*Virgil is a liar.*~~

    Virgil said he sent money to get the car fixed but he didn't. Mama is mad as anything. (What else is new? Ha Ha)

    That girl with the bracelet (her name is Loretta) asked me to teach her my yo-yo tricks. Maybe I will.

    ~~*I found her poodle dog pin.*~~

I ate all the cookies you sent. They were good.
Give Barney a hug.

> *Your friend,*
> *Kirby*

"Oh, yoo-hoo, Kirby."

Aggie shuffled toward him in her big yellow boots.

Kirby stuffed the letter into the box and clamped the lid on.

"I was wondering if maybe you'd like a little job," Aggie said.

Kirby shrugged.

"Maybe," he said.

"I could use some help cleaning out that storage room over by the office," Aggie said.

"Okay."

"I'll pay you, of course."

"You don't have to," Kirby said.

"Naw, I'm paying you." Aggie gave him a little push. "Shoot, you'll be wantin' a raise after you get a look at that room."

◈   ◈   ◈

Kirby wiped sweat off the back of his neck with a paper towel and pulled another dusty box off the shelf in the storage room. Aggie sat in a lawn chair outside the door.

Kirby was supposed to hold up each thing in the box for Aggie to see and then she would say *Keep, Sell, Give Away*, or *Toss*. Then he would put it into the right pile.

The trouble was, instead of saying *Keep, Sell, Give Away*, or *Toss*, Aggie would say, "My land's sakes alive, I'd forgotten all about that." Or, "Well, I'll be a saint in heaven, I thought I gave that to the paperboy." Or "Oh, bless me. I got that when me and Harold went to Charlotte to see his brother Ed."

Sometimes she would tell a long story. Like about how she had bought all those paper napkins at the flea market and figured they could use them in the bathrooms and save on the laundry bill, but Harold thought she had plumb lost her mind, so then he got some little ole tea towels real cheap and used a marker to write *Sleepy Time Motel* on them, but the writing wasn't very good and then it all came off in the washing machine anyway and then . . .

Kirby tried to listen.

He really, really tried to listen.

And he tried to be still while he was trying to listen.

But it was hard.

Now he was opening about the hundredth box, and the *Keep* pile was getting bigger and bigger, and there was nothing at all in the *Toss* pile.

Kirby reached in the box and took out a brown envelope. Inside the envelope was a frayed cloth patch. A round blue patch with a silver star and gold wings. He held it up for Aggie to see.

She drew in her breath and clasped her hands together.

"Well, would you look at that," she said, holding out a trembling hand to take the patch. She squinted down at it, turning it over and over, rubbing the front of it.

"What is it?" Kirby said.

"Harold got that in the war," she said, tracing the gold wings with a crooked finger. "It's from the Army Air Forces. That's what Harold was in. The Army Air Forces. Back in the war."

"Wow," Kirby said.

Aggie chuckled. Then she held the patch out to Kirby. "Here," she said. "You keep it."

Kirby shook his head. "Naw."

Aggie jabbed the patch at him. "Go on," she said. "Take it. Harold would've been tickled pink for you to have that."

Kirby eyed the patch. "Really?"

"Sure."

Kirby took the patch from Aggie. A real war patch! He wished his brother, Ace, could see this.

"Thanks," he said, tucking the patch into his shirt pocket.

"You're welcome," Aggie said.

Kirby pulled more things out of the box. A bowling trophy. Binoculars. A red plaid thermos. A hunting knife in a mildewed leather case. A clock with a cardinal on the front.

And then the rumble of a truck made him and Aggie stop what they were doing and look out at the parking lot.

"Who in the world could that be?" Aggie said.

Loretta

"Aren't we lucky, Marvin?" Loretta's mother patted Loretta's knee.

Her father nodded and said, "Yep."

Loretta forced a little smile.

They had gone for a drive, pulling over at all the lookout spots to see the view. Sometimes they put a quarter in the telescope and looked at the roads and cars and souvenir shops miles and miles away.

They had stopped at a roadside stand and bought boiled peanuts and saltwater taffy.

They had picked blackberries to take back to everyone at the Sleepy Time Motel.

But Loretta wasn't having much fun.

She couldn't stop thinking about the poodle dog pin.

Where had her other mother gotten it?

Had it been a gift, or had she bought it herself?

Had she seen it there in the store and just had to have it?

Had she worn it every day or only on special days?

And where was it now?

Loretta helped her mother clear off the picnic table, wrapping up the bologna and cheese and putting them back in the cooler.

Then they all climbed into the van and headed back to the Sleepy Time Motel. Now that the rain had stopped, the afternoon sun was peeking out from behind the clouds. Loretta held her face near the window, letting the cool mountain air blow her hair.

Maybe when she got back to the motel, Willow and Kirby would help her look for the pin.

Maybe Aggie had found it by now.

Or maybe it was gone forever.

Aggie

Aggie pushed herself up out of the lawn chair outside the storage room and followed Kirby across the parking lot to the roadside.

She read the words on the side of the truck parked there.

ALL-AMERICAN SIGN COMPANY.

Her feet kept moving but her heart stopped.

At least, it *felt* like her heart stopped. She clutched at Harold's old brown sweater. Her head was spinning. Her ears were ringing.

Clyde Dover was saying something.

To *her*?

Yes.

Clyde Dover was saying something to her.

He was grinning.

He was pointing.

Aggie shook her head, trying to clear the ringing in her ears.

". . . that surprise I told you about," is what Clyde Dover was saying.

Aggie made her eyes focus on the shiny new sign propped against the side of the truck.

MOUNTAINVIEW INN.

"Oh . . . well . . ." Aggie said.

Just those two words.

What else could she say?

Aggie felt herself leave.

Not her real self.

Not her achy old self standing there in the parking lot.

But her *inside* self.

Her happy young self who had met Harold at the magazine rack in the back of Walgreens Drugstore in Shelby, North Carolina, and had loved him right away.

Her inside self drifted right up off the ground and into the breezy mountain air and watched the scene taking place down there at the Sleepy Time Motel.

Here is what her inside self saw from way up there above the ground:

Clyde Dover, pointing at the shiny new motel sign and beaming at everyone.

Kirby, hopping around, splashing muddy water, fiddling with his yo-yo, tossing gravel into the road.

Willow, slumped in the rocking chair in front of Room 10.

Kirby's mother, Darlene, flicking a cigarette into the ditch by the road.

Dear little Ugly, swishing his scrawny tail back and forth across the wet grass.

The Murphys' white van bouncing across the parking lot and stopping in front of Room 6.

Loretta, jumping out and dashing over to join the others, that charm bracelet of hers jingle-jangling as she ran.

Loretta's parents, climbing out of the van, holding hands and smiling after Loretta like she was an angel come right down from heaven.

And last . . .

The two men from the sign company, grunting as they dug and pulled and dug and pulled until the Sleepy Time Motel sign came right up out of the ground.

When the doors of the truck slammed with a bang, Aggie's inside self fell from the sky above the motel and landed with a crash right inside her achy old self standing there by the road.

"Oh . . . well . . ." she said. "That's it, then."

She scooped up Ugly, wrapping him in the folds of Harold's old brown sweater. Most times, Ugly hated it when she did that, but this time, he leaned against her and purred.

She turned and headed back toward the motel. She dropped into a chair by the office door, settled Ugly on her lap, and closed her eyes.

"Want some taffy?"

Aggie opened her eyes. Loretta was sitting on the sidewalk in front of her.

Aggie smiled. She didn't have the heart to say *No, taffy gets stuck in my dentures.* So she took a piece of the gooey candy wrapped in waxed paper and tucked it into her pocket.

After Loretta said goodbye and skipped away, Aggie watched the sun sink behind the mountains—and the new motel sign glowing bright against the darkening sky.

Kirby walked along the side of the road, kicking a rusty soda can ahead of him. It bounced and clanged on the steamy hot asphalt. The early morning fog still hung over the treetops in the distance.

Every now and then a car whizzed by, stirring up a warm breeze. Then the air would settle back down.

Thick.

Still.

Hot.

The puddles along the roadside were drying up fast, the red mud turning back into hard-packed clay.

Kirby didn't know how far he had walked. After a while,

he went down a side street off the main highway, passing several houses, some gravel roads, a trailer park.

Eventually, he left the road and pushed through the weeds and low-hanging branches until he came to a clearing. Along one side were big, flat rocks with sparkly flecks of silver that glittered in the sunlight. Kirby climbed onto the rocks and lay back, feeling the heat seep right through his clothes to his skin.

He looked up at the clouds, studying their shapes. One looked like an elephant. Another like an angel with outspread wings. Another one looked like stairs. Soft, cottony stairs.

Kirby imagined himself walking up those stairs.

Up and up and up.

To where?

Anywhere would be good.

Anywhere was better than here, next to the winding mountain road that led to the school for losers like him.

He took Loretta's pin out of his pocket and studied it. He tilted it back and forth. The tiny rhinestones sparkled in the sun.

He put the pin back in his pocket and stayed up there in the clouds all morning.

☽ ☽ ☽

When he got back to the motel, Room 1 was empty. His mother was probably checking the mail again, looking for the money that Virgil had supposedly sent. Their broken-down car had been towed to the Texaco gas station a few days ago, but the mechanic wouldn't fix it until he got some money.

Kirby took the shoebox that Burla had given him out to the picnic table. He fished through the stuff inside until he found the folded-up postcard.

Greetings from the Great Smoky Mountains

He crossed out *the Great Smoky Mountains* and wrote *Nowhere.*

Greetings from Nowhere

He turned the card over and thought about who to write and what he should say.

Dear Burla, I miss you.

Hey, Ace, I got a war patch.

Dear Virgil, I don't miss you.

Dear Dad, Thanks for nothing.

Kirby looked up at the sound of someone running toward him on the gravel parking lot.

"Hey, Kirby!" Loretta called. She was wearing a vest with long, leathery fringe and a sheriff's badge.

"Where've you been?" she said.

Kirby put his arm over the postcard.

Loretta sat at the picnic table beside him. "We went to Maggie Valley and rode a train," she said.

Kirby pushed the postcard up under the box and went over to the swimming pool. He jumped down into the shallow end, ran to the deep end, trotted in circles around the drain a few times, and then climbed up the ladder. He bounced on the diving board. It made *boing, boing* noises that echoed in the still summer air.

"The train went through a tunnel," Loretta said, sitting on the edge of the pool. "And then it stopped at a cowboy town."

"That's upid-stay," Kirby said. His brother, Ace, would have punched him for saying that. Or run off to tell Mama. He might have even cried.

But Loretta just kept on talking about that cowboy town and how she had a Buffalo Bill burger for lunch, and then out of the clear blue she said, "Will you help me look for my poodle dog pin tomorrow?"

Kirby stopped bouncing. "What?"

"Will you help me look for my poodle dog pin tomorrow?"

Kirby glanced at the sheriff's badge pinned to her fringed vest. He was thinking about telling her that she looked like an upid-stay aby-bay, but he didn't.

"Maybe," he said.

"We're gonna make s'mores on the barbecue grill tonight," Loretta said. "Wanna come?"

Kirby studied Loretta. Her freckly face. Her straight, dark hair held back with blue barrettes. "Okay," he said.

☾ ☾ ☾

Kirby slapped another mosquito and watched Loretta blow out her burning marshmallow.

Her parents sat in lawn chairs sipping beers. They called Loretta "LuLu" and hugged her a lot. They told Kirby to call them Irene and Marvin. They asked him questions nobody had ever asked him before. What was his favorite sport? Did he have a dog? How did he like the Smoky Mountains?

At first, Kirby had just mumbled a few words.

He liked baseball.

The Smoky Mountains were okay.

But after a while, he started talking more. He told Irene about the bird's nest on his windowsill last spring. How he had seen the eggs hatch and he still had some of the broken shells in his dresser drawer back home. He told Marvin about the time he'd won a baseball bat signed by the Atlanta Braves when he came closest to guessing the number of pennies in a pickle jar at the 7-Eleven.

He even told them about Burla. Her teapot wallpaper. Her thumbprint cookies. Her old dog, Barney.

He showed Loretta a couple of yo-yo tricks. He tried to teach her Hop the Fence but she couldn't get the hang of it. Everyone laughed when she got all tangled up in the string.

Even him.

After a while, Willow and her dad came out and joined them at the barbecue grill. Willow told them Aggie had a headache and had gone to bed early.

Kirby let Willow use his coat hanger to roast her marshmallow.

He did some more yo-yo tricks and everyone clapped.

When his mother hollered over from Room 1 that he needed to get hisself inside, everyone seemed disappointed.

"Ask her if you can stay a little longer," Loretta said.

"Maybe tomorrow we can see if there's any fish in that creek back yonder," Marvin said.

And Willow, who hardly ever said anything to him, said, "Thank you for the coat hanger."

As Kirby trotted over to Room 1, he could feel that poodle pin in his pocket getting heavier and heavier.

He glanced back at the folks sitting out there by the barbecue grill. The folks who had been so nice to him.

Then he went inside, letting the door slam shut behind him.

"Maybe I should keep these," Aggie said to Ugly.

She looked down at Harold's old plaid slippers in her lap.

"Remember that time he forgot he had them on and wore them to Sandy Ganner's piano recital?"

Aggie smiled at Ugly.

Ugly purred.

Aggie sighed.

"I don't know," she said. "Maybe we won't like that condominium in Raleigh."

She put the slippers on top of the pile of clothes on her bed. Then she pushed aside the curtain over the doorway to the office and peered in.

Willow wasn't there.

Aggie was surprised how disappointed she felt. Funny how quickly you got used to having someone around.

She studied the office. That new paint color looked nice. Brightened the place up a bit.

But where were the cup hooks?

The postcard rack was easier to reach over there in that corner.

But where were the complimentary maps?

"Well, good morning!"

Aggie jumped.

Clyde Dover stepped into the office, carrying a steaming cup of coffee.

Willow trailed behind him, sipping orange juice through a straw. "Has the mail come yet?" she said.

Aggie looked over at the basket where Clayton Underwood always left the mail.

"Not yet," she said.

"I was thinking maybe you ought to go ahead and change your mailing address," Mr. Dover said. "You know, so you won't miss out on anything."

Aggie chuckled. "Only thing I'd miss out on is bills and bad news."

"Guess what," Mr. Dover said. "There might be a tour group coming here in a few days."

"Really?"

A tour group! Aggie felt a little twitch of excitement. "We

used to have tour groups staying here all the time," she said. "Well, not all the time. But once in a while."

Aggie looked out the screen door to the parking lot, picturing the Greyhound bus full of folks from up in Gatlinburg or over in Chattanooga. One time a school bus came. A school bus full of children from some school in Charlotte. Harold had entertained them with magic tricks out by the pool. The pool had had water in it then. Clear, sparkling water.

"It's not for sure yet," Mr. Dover said. "But I've been talking to this travel agent over in Asheville, and I'm waiting to hear."

Aggie adjusted her glasses and studied Mr. Dover. He looked proud. And hopeful. And a little nervous.

Just the way she and Harold must have looked all those years ago when the motel was brand-new.

"Of course, I got a lot of work to do on some of them rooms," Mr. Dover said. "Carpets need cleaning. A couple of window blinds are broke. And that showerhead in Room 8 needs replacing."

Aggie nodded. "That dang thing never did work right," she said.

"I thought I'd have time to get the lawn chairs washed, but now I've gotta see about the light fixture in Room 3."

And then Willow's quiet little voice chimed in, "Maybe Aggie should stay and help us."

Aggie looked at Willow.

Willow looked at her father.

Her father looked down at his shoes.

And the room filled up with silence.

Mr. Dover cleared his throat.

"Well . . ." Aggie said.

"Those rooms won't be ready if that tour bus comes," Willow said. "And then nobody will want to stay and then—"

"Willow," Mr. Dover said, "why don't you go put them tissue boxes in the rooms, like I told you to."

Aggie watched Willow turn and push the screen door open like it was made out of cement. "I reckon I better go water my begonias," she said.

❋ ❋ ❋

Outside, the sun streamed through big fluffy clouds in a blue, blue sky. Everything seemed to glitter. The gravel in the parking lot. The still-dewy grass around the flagpole.

Aggie took a deep breath.

"Honeysuckle," she said out loud.

"Hey, Aggie!"

Loretta was running up the sidewalk toward her.

"Hey there," Aggie said. "Where y'all going today?"

"Tuckaleechee Caverns," Loretta said.

"Oh, you're gonna love it there," Aggie said. "Me and Harold used to go there all the time."

She snapped a dry, brown leaf off a begonia and tucked it into the pocket of her apron. "Some of those cave explorers used to stay here at the motel."

"Spelunkers," Loretta said.

"What?"

"Spelunkers. That's what cave explorers are called."

"Well, ain't you smart?" Aggie hung her watering can on the hook by the outdoor spigot.

"I read it in the AAA book," Loretta said.

Aggie dropped into a plastic lawn chair and wiped her neck with Harold's handkerchief.

"It's gonna be a scorcher today," she said.

Loretta sat beside her. "Which place on my bracelet do you think we should visit next?" she said, holding her arm out and jangling her bracelet.

Aggie studied the little silver charms.

The starfish.

The cowboy boot.

The Statue of Liberty.

"Hmmm," she said. "Well, I reckon if you don't mind big cities, the Statue of Liberty would be a sight to see. And I imagine you'd like Disney World." She jiggled the Mickey Mouse charm. "But me? I'd go to Niagara Falls."

Loretta looked at her bracelet and cocked her head. "Or maybe Texas!" she said, pointing to the cowboy boot.

Just then a car pulled into the parking lot. Clayton Underwood.

Aggie pushed herself up and went out to meet him.

"Hey," she said.

"Hey back at ya," Clayton said. "You hit the jackpot today."

He handed her a stack of envelopes.

"Uh-oh," Aggie said. "Who did I forget to pay now?"

Clayton chuckled. "You got them boxes packed up yet?" he said.

Aggie felt a little flutter in her stomach. Not the good kind of flutter like you get on Christmas morning, but the bad kind, like you get when you think of something scary.

The flutter moved to her hands, making them tremble. Making them drop the envelopes.

Then it moved up to her face, making her chin quiver. "Um, not yet," she said.

"You okay?" Clayton said, squinting up at her from under his camouflage hunter's cap.

Aggie gathered the envelopes scattered in the gravel. She nodded.

"Gimme a shout when them boxes are ready, then," Clayton said, tipping his cap and pulling out of the parking lot.

It was nearly lunchtime, and Aggie was still sitting in the lawn chair outside her room. Ugly lay curled up in her lap.

Willow and her father had gone to the hardware store.

Loretta and her parents were off to Tuckaleechee Caverns.

Kirby had fixed up that old bicycle in the shed and gone for a ride somewhere. His mother had walked down to the convenience store to pick up a few things.

Aggie had been so lost in thought, she'd forgotten all about the stack of envelopes that Clayton had brought until she spotted them there on the rusty metal table beside her. She picked them up and leafed through them.

The telephone bill.

The water bill.

A small white envelope addressed to Kirby's mother. *Darlene Tanner*.

"Well, look at this, Ugly," Aggie said. "This is for Kirby's mother. Maybe it's the money she's been waiting for. You know, to get the car fixed."

There was a bill from the soda machine company, marked *Urgent. Second Request.*

On the bottom of the pile was a large manila envelope addressed to Willow.

Aggie grinned.

"This one's for Willow," she said to Ugly.

She clutched the envelope against her chest. "I sure hope this is from that mother of hers she's been pining for so much, don't you?"

Ugly twitched his ear.

Aggie studied the envelope, running her fingers lightly across the front.

Then she looked up at the sky and said, "Harold, I don't know if you got any pull up there or not, but if you do . . ." She jabbed a finger at the envelope. ". . . let this be from Willow's mama."

Aggie gathered the envelopes, nudged Ugly off her lap, and shuffled up the sidewalk to her room.

But just before going inside, she looked up at the sky again and said, "By the way, her name is Dorothy."

Willow stared out the window of the pickup truck, thinking about what to say.

Should she say, *Daddy, please let Aggie stay at the motel*?

Or maybe, *Aggie's sad about leaving the motel, so I think she should stay*?

How about, *We should ask Aggie to stay and help us get ready for the tour group*?

She looked over at her father. He hummed as he drove, his elbow propped up on the open window.

"Daddy?" she said.

No answer.

"Daddy?" she said a little louder.

Her father kept his eyes on the road and said, "Hmmm?"

"I was thinking, well, I thought . . . I mean, maybe . . ."
Willow looked down at her lap, trying hard to find just the
right words. "Don't you think we oughtta ask Aggie to stay
at the motel instead of going to live with her cousin in
Raleigh?" Willow closed her eyes and waited.

Nothing.

She glanced at her father.

He kept his eyes on the road.

Willow could feel her heart beating. Thump. Thump.
Thump.

She tried to send a mental message over to her father.

Say yes.

Say yes.

Say yes.

But when her father answered, he didn't say yes.

He said something mean.

"Willow," he said, "you can't give a home to every stray
dog in this world."

Willow felt a wave of mad run through her from the tip
of her pink plastic sandals to the top of her head.

"Aggie's not a stray dog!" she hollered, making her father
jump.

He pulled the truck over to the side of the road and
turned to face her. His jaw twitched. His eyes narrowed.

"The motel doesn't belong to Aggie anymore," he said. He ran his hand over his buzz-cut hair. "The motel belongs to us."

"But Aggie *lives* there," Willow said.

"She has a new place to live now."

"She won't like it there."

"You don't know that, Willow."

"Uh-huh." Willow nodded. "Besides, she knows a lot about motels. And she can help us do stuff. And she—"

"Willow." Her father set his face in that hard way that told Willow he was through talking.

Then he pulled the truck back into the road and stared ahead like Willow wasn't even there.

⊘ ⊘ ⊘

As soon as they got back to the motel, Willow jumped out of the truck and ran over to the picnic table. She climbed up on it and sat down, hugging her knees. She wished she were back in Hailey. If she were back in Hailey, she would go out to the little patch of weeds that used to be the flowers that Dorothy grew. She would stay there forever and never talk to anyone except for maybe Maggie, once in a while.

Willow looked up at the sound of someone walking across the gravel parking lot.

Crunch, crunch, crunch.

Aggie waved an envelope.

Ugly sauntered along behind her.

"This came for you today," Aggie said, handing the envelope to Willow.

Willow clutched the envelope with both hands. "It worked!" she said. "The cobweb worked!"

She reminded Aggie about how Dorothy believed that if you walked into a cobweb, you'd get a letter from someone you loved. Then she told Aggie about the cobweb in the garden.

"Well, I'll be . . ." Aggie said.

Willow opened the envelope and peered inside. More envelopes. She dumped them out onto the picnic table. Along with the envelopes was a scrap of paper torn from a spiral notebook.

Dear Willow,

These letters came for you. I hope you are doing good and that you like that motel. I am fine. It has been hot here. Maggie says hi.

Love,
Grannie Dover

Willow picked up one of the envelopes. There on the front was her mother's loopy handwriting, just like on the calendar.

Willow's stomach fluttered with excitement. "It's from Dorothy!" she said, clasping the envelope against her heart.

Aggie grinned. Then she looked up at the sky and said, "Thank you, Harold."

☉ ☉ ☉

Willow read every letter twice.

Each one started the same way:

Dear Willow,
  I miss you so much . . .

Each one ended the same way:

I love you very much.
  Mama

Willow folded the letters carefully and tucked them back inside the big envelope. Then she ran across the parking lot to where Aggie sat outside the office.

She told Aggie everything that Dorothy had written in the letters.

How she was down in Savannah with her sister Sarah, in a house next to a church where Sarah's husband was the preacher.

How she was working in a doctor's office, answering the phone.

How she missed Willow more than anything and thought about her every day.

Aggie put her hand on Willow's knee. "Ain't that nice?" she said, giving Willow a little pat.

Willow nodded. "And pretty soon, I can go and visit her in Savannah," she said.

◑ ◑ ◑

When Loretta and Kirby came back, Willow showed them the envelope full of letters. She told them all about Dorothy and the house with the preacher and the job at the doctor's office. She even read them one of the letters.

Loretta ran to get her AAA book that had a map of Georgia so they could look for Savannah. Willow circled it with a blue marker. Loretta let her tear out the page and keep it.

Kirby didn't say much, but he let Willow try some of his yo-yo tricks.

Around the Corner.

Dizzy Baby.

They looked for Loretta's pin for a while, Loretta leading them all around the motel, Kirby trailing behind, jumping over stuff, touching everything.

Then they went out to the swimming pool and sat in a

circle around the drain and said stuff to each other in pig Latin.

Loretta even sang a pig Latin song.

Ow-ray, ow-ray, ow-ray our-yay oat-bay . . .

When Ugly appeared at the edge of the pool and peered down at them with his one eye, Willow tried to coax him to join them, patting the cement beside her and calling, "Here, kitty, kitty." But Ugly just blinked.

Then Aggie appeared, calling down to them, "How's the water?"

They all laughed.

"Come on in," Loretta called.

"Yeah, come on in," Willow called.

"Lawd, I might not ever get up out of there if I came down them steps," Aggie said.

"We'll teach you pig Latin," Loretta said. "Ome-cay own-day ere-hay."

So Aggie joined them down there by the drain. She sat on the crumbling cement with her scrawny legs stretched out in front of her and Ugly in her lap.

They stayed there till it was almost dark, singing pig Latin songs and doing yo-yo tricks, while lightning bugs flickered all around them.

Loretta

Loretta pinned the sheriff's badge on her T-shirt and headed outside to show her rubies to somebody. That ruby mine over in Cherokee had been her very favorite place in the Smoky Mountains. She had liked it even better than Dollywood.

Aggie was sitting out by the office. Loretta ran over and showed her the tiny rubies in a plastic sandwich bag.

"And guess what else," Loretta said.

"What?"

"I saw a charm just like this one in a souvenir shop there." Loretta held her arm up and pointed to the little bear charm.

"Well, I'll be . . ." Aggie said.

"That means maybe my other mother was right there in that very same shop." Loretta wiggled her arm, making the bracelet jingle. "Maybe she went to the ruby mine."

"Maybe," Aggie said.

Just then Kirby came out of Room 1. He walked across the parking lot toward the swimming pool, his hands jammed into the pockets of his jeans.

"Come see what I got," Loretta called to him.

He shook his head and kept walking.

"I got real rubies," Loretta called.

Kirby kept walking. When he got to the pool, he jumped down the steps and ran into the deep end, disappearing from view.

"Now, what do you suppose is the matter with him?" Aggie said.

"Let's go see." Loretta ran out to the pool and peered over the edge.

"What's the matter?" she said.

Kirby was sitting down by the drain. He made squiggly lines on the dirty cement with a stick. "Virgil sent the money to get the car fixed," he said.

"That's good," Loretta said.

"I suppose."

"So now y'all can go on up to that school," Loretta said.

"Whatever." Kirby snapped the stick in half and tossed the pieces up by the diving board.

When Aggie joined Loretta at the edge of the pool, Loretta told her about Virgil and the money. "So now they can get their car fixed and Kirby can go on up to that school," she said.

"Oh," Aggie said.

Loretta pulled the sandwich bag out of her pocket. "These are real rubies." She waved the bag at Kirby. "You want one?"

Kirby shook his head, making his red hair flop back and forth.

Loretta watched him, sitting there so still and quiet at the bottom of the pool. She tried to think of something to say that would make him bounce on the diving board or race around the drain or hop up the steps.

But she couldn't.

"I'm gonna show these rubies to Willow," she said, and ran off toward the office.

Willow was coming out of Room 8, carrying a bucket of cleaning supplies.

"Hey," Loretta called, skipping over to her.

"Hey." Willow put the bucket down and pushed her hair out of her face.

"Whatcha doin'?" Loretta said.

"Cleaning."

"Look at my rubies." Loretta showed Willow the plastic sandwich bag with the tiny rubies in the bottom.

"Those are nice," Willow said.

"My other mother was there at that very same ruby mine," Loretta said.

"Really?"

"Well, maybe." Loretta folded the plastic bag and tucked it back into her pocket. "You want to play flashlight tag tonight? We can ask Kirby, too."

Willow shook her head. "I have to help Daddy," she said. "A tour group is coming this weekend, and there's a lot of stuff to do."

Willow picked up the bucket and disappeared into Room 7.

◉   ◉   ◉

That night Loretta sat with her parents and Aggie out by the pool. Every now and then, a car went by, sending a beam of headlights across the front of the motel. Moths fluttered around the new sign glowing in the darkness.

MOUNTAINVIEW INN.

Under that, VACANCY flashed in bright red.

On and off.

On and off.

They all looked up at the sound of someone walking across the parking lot. Clyde Dover joined them, dropping into a lawn chair with a big, heavy sigh.

"When does that tour group get here?" Aggie said.

He let out another sigh. "They're not coming," he said.

"Why not?"

"I called that travel agent over in Asheville and told him to forget it. There's no way I can have this place ready in time."

Loretta jumped up out of her chair. "We can help," she said.

Mr. Dover chuckled and shook his head. "It would take a miracle to get this place in shape in time," he said. "There's carpets to clean and—"

"I can do that," Loretta's mother said.

"—showers to fix," Mr. Dover went on.

"Shoot, Clyde," Loretta's father said, "I *am* a plumber, you know."

Mr. Dover ran his hand over his head and sighed. "There's curtains to be hung and—"

"I can do that," Aggie piped in.

"There's all them weeds in the parking lot that's gotta be pulled up—"

"I can do that," a voice called out of the darkness. Kirby appeared in the glow of the sign, flinging his yo-yo down with a whir and catching it with a slap.

Behind him, Willow walked in her tiptoe way, in her pink plastic sandals, and sat on the steps of the pool.

Before long, everybody was naming all the stuff they

could do to help, and Clyde Dover was starting to perk up a bit.

They could start bright and early in the morning.

Loretta's father would pick up the carpet shampooer.

Aggie would look for her sewing kit and hem those curtains.

Loretta and Willow would wash all the lawn chairs.

Loretta's mother would call and make sure the soda machine got filled.

They would paint the doors and fix the broken windows and change the lightbulbs.

They talked late into the night, making lists of chores and who would do them, while Loretta danced around the flagpole, shining her flashlight up into the sky.

Dear Burla,

Loretta gave me a real ruby.

Virgil sent the money to fix the car, so I guess I will be at that school soon.

How is Barney? Tell him I said woof woof.

Your friend,
Kirby

Kirby folded the letter and sealed it inside the envelope. Then he flopped back on the bed and stared up at the water-stained ceiling. A fly buzzed around the lightbulb up there.

His mother was humming in the bathroom. He could

hear the *pssssst* of her hairspray. Could smell the sticky sweetness of it.

"So you be ready in case I call, okay?" she said, padding out of the bathroom in her bare feet.

She slapped his leg. "I'm talking to you," she said.

"I hear you." Kirby kept his eyes on the ceiling.

"Then answer me." His mother sat on the bed and put her sandals on. "If the car's ready, we're outta here," she said.

"Whatever." Kirby kept his eyes on that buzzing fly.

"I'll call up yonder to that school before we leave," his mother said.

"Whatever."

He closed his eyes and stayed real still until his mother left the room, slamming the door behind her. Then he jumped off the bed and peered through the slats of the window blinds. He watched his mother march across the parking lot and disappear up the road.

When he went outside, the sun was just peeking over the top of the mountains. The air was cool and damp. He could hear the eighteen-wheelers roaring up the interstate on the other side of the ridge behind the motel.

"Good morning, son," Clyde Dover called from the office door. "You still up for doing that weeding?" he said.

"Yessir."

So Mr. Dover showed Kirby where the rusty old wheelbarrow was and gave him a hoe with a broken handle, and Kirby set to work.

He chopped at the hard red dirt. He pulled weeds and tossed them into the wheelbarrow.

Chop.

Pull.

Toss.

All morning long.

And the whole time, that poodle dog pin burned, burned, burned in his pocket.

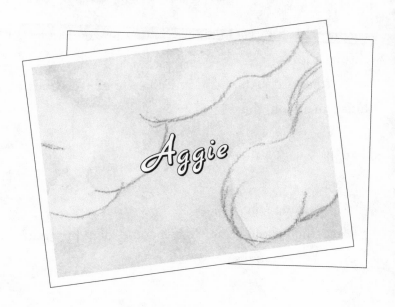

Aggie dropped raisins into her oatmeal and talked to Ugly in pig Latin.

Ood-gay orning-may.

Ant-way ome-say una-tay?

Then she pushed aside the sponges and spray bottles and garbage bags under the kitchen sink, looking for the laundry detergent.

Ugly watched her with his one eye, the tip of his tail twitching on the worn orange carpet.

"Maybe I left it in the laundry room," Aggie said.

She gathered a bundle of towels and headed outside. Shuffling up the sidewalk in her bedroom slippers, she took a deep breath. The air smelled sweet and clean.

And then something hit her.

Hard.

Not a real thing she could touch.

But a feeling.

A feeling caused by a thought.

This was the thought: *These mountains are a part of me, like my arm or my hand or my heart. And in just a few days, I will be leaving them forever.*

Aggie sat in the chair outside of Room 3 and clutched the bundle of towels against her.

Out by the water spigot, Loretta and Willow were washing plastic lawn chairs and singing a song about finding a peanut.

Loretta was wearing her cowboy vest over her bathing suit. Her jangly charm bracelet danced up and down her arm as she washed. Willow wore her pink plastic sandals and held her chin up in the air while she sang.

Aggie smiled, forgetting all about the thought that had caused the feeling that had hit her hard.

Then she gathered up the towels and headed on over to the laundry room.

☾ ☾ ☾

The morning seemed to fly by. Aggie hung curtains in Room 8 and changed lightbulbs in Room 3. She washed the coffee mugs and put extra soap in every room. She held the stool while Loretta's mother fixed the window blinds in Room 7. She showed Clyde Dover where to turn off the main water valve so he and Loretta's father could work on the plumbing.

Out in the parking lot, Kirby tossed weeds into the wheelbarrow, while Loretta and Willow dragged the clean chairs back out to the pool.

Birds hopped around the filled-up bird feeder and the flag fluttered in the breeze at the top of the flagpole.

The little motel was beginning to hum.

Willow watched her father spread grape jelly on bread. He had made a little kitchen on top of the dresser in their room. A toaster. A microwave oven. A tiny refrigerator. A milk crate filled with saltine crackers, bread, peanut butter, cans of soup.

"How many people are coming in the tour group?" Willow asked, pulling the crust off her cheese sandwich.

"About nine or ten, I think." Her father tossed the jelly knife into the bathroom sink.

"It sure is nice of Aggie to help us," Willow said. "You know, since the motel's not hers anymore."

Her father nodded, humming as he studied the To Do list on his clipboard.

Willow got a little fluttery feeling.

Her father wasn't closed up tight anymore. She could tell he had opened a tiny crack.

More than anything, she wanted to say, *Daddy, please let Aggie stay here with us.*

But she knew she had to be careful. That tiny crack could snap shut at any minute.

Like a mousetrap.

Snap!

So she said, "I'm going to look for Loretta."

Willow ran to Room 6. When she got there, Loretta came out and handed her a paper cup full of blackberries.

They raced out to the swimming pool and sat on the steps, eating their blackberries and talking.

About school.

About their friends.

About their favorite cereal.

About whether Loretta should go to Niagara Falls or Disney World.

About what they wanted for their birthdays.

And about Dorothy.

Willow loved how easy Loretta was to talk to. Even easier than Maggie. But the best thing was that no matter what Willow said, Loretta always had a good idea about it.

Like, when Willow told her she wanted to go visit Dorothy down in Savannah, Loretta said she should take one of those maps from the office with her and put a big red circle around the spot where the motel was.

"That way," Loretta said, "she can come visit *you* and she won't get lost."

And when Willow told Loretta that Dorothy's birthday was July 27, Loretta squealed, "Her birthday's in *July*?"

Willow nodded.

Loretta grabbed Willow's shoulders and gave her a little shake.

"That's *ruby*!" she said.

"What's ruby?"

"*July.* The birthstone for July is *ruby*," Loretta said. "You can send her one of those rubies I got in Cherokee!"

Willow could hardly believe Loretta was going to give her one of those shiny little rubies she had found up in the ruby mine in Cherokee. She made up her mind right then and there that she was going to give Loretta one of her china horses. Maybe the gray mare with the flowing white mane. That one had a tiny baby horse that went with it. Willow might even give her the baby horse, too.

It was nearly noon when Aggie came out to the parking lot
and gave Kirby a sandwich. The morning mist had burned
off and the air was still and hot.

Kirby's hands were blistered and his shoulders hurt. He
had filled up that old wheelbarrow about a hundred times,
making trip after trip around back to dump the weeds into
the burn pile by the garden.

"I got sweet tea, too," Aggie said, holding up a thermos.

Kirby followed her out to the picnic table. He wiped his
dirty hands on his shirttail and sat next to her.

"Ain't that a beautiful sight?" Aggie said, gazing out at the
gray-green treetops in the distance. "I just love these mountains."

Kirby nodded.

He was on his second cheese sandwich when Aggie said, "What's that?"

She shuffled over to the edge of the grassy patch by the flagpole and reached for something up under the bushes.

She came back and sat next to Kirby.

"Where in the world did this come from?" she said.

Kirby looked down at what she was holding.

A postcard.

A postcard of the Smoky Mountains.

A postcard that used to say *Greetings from the Great Smoky Mountains.*

But now it was a postcard that said *Greetings from Nowhere.*

The word *Nowhere* was scrawled across the front in big angry letters.

Aggie's hands were shaking.

Kirby's heart was pounding.

"Thank you for the sandwiches," he said.

He hurried back out to the parking lot to chop weeds in the hard, dry earth.

He glanced over at Aggie. She slipped the postcard into the pocket of her apron and cleared the paper cups off the picnic table.

He kept chopping.

Chop.

Chop.

Chop.

That poodle dog pin so heavy in his pocket.

And then Aggie was standing next to him. "It must've been my lucky day when that car of yours broke down," she said.

Kirby stopped weeding and looked at her.

"I mean, besides being a dern good weeder and a champion yo-yo-er, you're a fine young man," she said.

For a flicker of a minute, Kirby felt like he was in the wrong life. Like somehow he had gotten plucked out of Kirby Tanner's life and plopped right down into somebody else's.

Somebody who didn't have to steal and lie to make people notice him.

Somebody who was a fine young man.

And in the next flicker of a minute, Kirby wished he hadn't kept that pin that was so special to Loretta, who was always nice to him.

And he wished he hadn't written that angry word about the Smoky Mountains that Aggie loved so much.

He wished he really *was* a fine young man.

Loretta

Loretta dumped the things out of the box and spread them on the bed. She refolded the blue handkerchief embroidered with a *P*. She opened the silver pocket watch engraved with *WKL*. She smoothed out the creases on the hummingbird picture.

"Mama?" she said.

Her mother looked up from her magazine. "Hmmm?"

"Do you think my other mother would be mad at me for losing her poodle dog pin?"

Her mother put down the magazine and gathered Loretta in her arms. Loretta pressed her face against her mother's warm, soft body and breathed in her talcum powder smell.

"Lulu," her mother said, "I think she'd know you're the best little girl in the whole world. That's what I think."

"But what about the pin?"

Her mother took her by the shoulders. "I think she'd know that people make mistakes and that accidents happen," she said. "Don't you?"

Loretta shrugged. "I guess."

Her mother put her arm around her and led her over to the window. "Look at those mountains, Lulu," she said.

Loretta looked out at the gray-green mountains. A layer of smoky clouds hovered over the tops of them.

"Your other mother looked out at those very same mountains," her mother said.

Loretta took in every inch of the scene outside the window, imagining her other mother seeing the very same thing.

The same pine trees.

The same puffy clouds.

The same winding roads.

And somewhere out there along the mountaintop, Loretta found a piece of herself. Like that last missing piece of a jigsaw puzzle, snapped into place with a sigh of satisfaction, making the picture whole.

Loretta hugged her mother and said, "I love you."

Then she wiggled her hand, making her charm bracelet

jingle up and down her arm, and said, "I'm gonna go take Willow one of my rubies."

○ ○ ○

Loretta skipped up the sidewalk toward the office. She peered through the screen door. Willow sat on a stool at the counter, watching the little television her father had put there that morning.

"I brought you a ruby," Loretta called through the screen door.

Willow jumped off the stool and came outside. They ran and sat on the picnic table. Loretta gave Willow the ruby and Willow gave Loretta the little china horses. The mama horse and the baby horse.

When the lightning bugs came out, Loretta and Willow took turns catching one, making a wish, and then letting it go again.

Then they sat on the steps of the swimming pool and looked around them at the little motel.

The lawn chairs, clean and tidy around the pool.

The parking lot without the weeds.

Room 3 with the freshly painted door.

Room 2 with the broken window fixed.

"Your motel looks nice," Loretta said.

Willow smiled. "Thank you," she said.

They sat there on the steps, shoulder to shoulder, and watched the sun disappear completely behind the mountains.

The MOUNTAINVIEW INN sign glowed.

VACANCY flashed on and off.

On and off.

Aggie put Harold's plaid slippers on top of the other things in the box.

"There," she said to Ugly.

Then she put on her old canvas sneakers and grabbed a hat (the big straw one she got in Florida) and went around back to the garden.

Ugly trotted along behind her.

Grasshoppers sprang up out of the weeds as she made her way to the tomato garden.

"Well, Harold," she said, "I'll be heading over to Evelyn's this week and . . ."

Aggie took a deep breath and closed her eyes. Then she continued. "I hope you don't mind if I gave that boy, Kirby, your patch from the war, but he seems kinda needy. You know? Seems like his kin are so busy waiting for him to do something bad that they miss out on him doing something good."

She picked a fat, green tomato worm off one of the plants and tossed it into the weeds.

"And Loretta. Lawd, that little thing is just a bundle of sunshine, skipping around here with that bracelet of hers jangling away."

Aggie chuckled. "You know, I think she came here to these mountains looking for a little piece of herself, and I have a feeling she found it."

Ugly rubbed against Aggie's legs, purring.

"And then there's Willow." Aggie smiled up at the sky. "Pining away for her mother and missing that love so much. Seems like most of what she needs is just a good hug once in a while." Aggie looked down at her dirty sneakers. "But then, never having children of my own, what do I know, right?"

She looked skyward again. "Oh, and thanks again for getting them letters to Willow. I knew I could count on you."

Then she went over and sat in the lawn chair at the edge of the garden and told Harold all about the tour group. How they'd be here any minute now. How they were coming on a bus from down in Atlanta.

Then she told him about all the things they had done to

spruce up the motel. The painting and hammering and washing and all.

"You should see it," she said. "But then"—she chuckled—"I reckon you can."

She pushed herself out of the chair and headed down the path out of the garden. But before she rounded the corner of the motel, she looked up at the mountain sky and said, "This has been one heck of a parade, ain't it, Harold?"

Willow made sure the guest book was on the counter and the coffee mugs were lined up and the little silver bell was ready in case one of their guests needed something. Then she looked out the office door for about the millionth time to see if the tour bus was there yet.

But it wasn't.

So she went outside to look for Aggie. She looked in the laundry room and out by the flagpole. Then she ran up the sidewalk past the rooms with the freshly painted doors and went along the path toward the garden. But before she rounded the corner, she heard someone talking.

Aggie.

Aggie talking to Harold.

Aggie saying, "This has been one heck of a parade, ain't it, Harold?"

And then Willow had a moment.

A lightbulb moment.

One of those moments when the light goes on with a *click* and everything is suddenly clearer than it had been the minute before.

Kirby stuffed his dirty T-shirts into the duffel bag and zipped it up.

"...better not be getting no calls from that school..." his mother was saying.

"...if you were more like Ace..."

"...I've tried and I've tried, but you..."

On and on and on.

His mother telling him all those things he already knew because he'd heard them so many times before.

"...ain't gonna tolerate your lying and..."

Kirby went outside and put his duffel bag in the backseat of their car.

And then a bus pulled into the parking lot, sending up

clouds of red dust as it came to a stop in front of the office.

The bus doors opened with a *hiss* and folks ambled down the steps and out into the parking lot, carrying backpacks and tote bags and cameras.

Mr. Dover rushed out of the office, grinning. He shook their hands and helped them with their bags and pointed out the ice machine and the soda machine and the laundry room.

Aggie came out and gave them each a map and introduced them to Ugly.

Willow stood just inside the office door with the guest book in her hand.

Kirby ran over to help.

Loretta

Loretta put the two little china horses into her box with all her other mother's earthly possessions.

"I'm going to go say goodbye to everyone," she said.

Her mother smiled and nodded as she folded clothes and put them into the opened suitcases on the bed.

Outside, a bus was pulling into the parking lot. A big bus with *Holiday Tours* on the side.

"The tour group!" Loretta squealed.

Everyone was scurrying around like ants. Mr. Dover and Aggie were showing folks to their rooms, unlocking the doors, opening the blinds, handing out extra soaps. Willow was making sure everyone had a pen to sign the guest book. Kirby was helping folks with their bags.

So Loretta ran over to help, too. She told the ladies in the tour group all about the spelunkers at Tuckaleechee Caverns. She told the men about the cowboy town over in Maggie Valley. And she showed everyone her rubies.

Willow looked down at the guest book opened on the counter.

Dave and Lillian Klinger from Belton, South Carolina
Ollie Branson from Athens, Georgia
Hattie Norris from Dayton, Ohio
Mr. Frank T. Dodd from Fairfax, Virginia
Mr. and Mrs. Godfrey Hix from Baltimore, Maryland
Augusta Russell from Cleveland, Mississippi
Felton Nisbet from Fountain Inn, South Carolina
Roy and Doris Gilmer from Cedar Bluff, Alabama

The motel would be full!

Willow and Aggie were going to hurry and clean Kirby's and Loretta's rooms after they left.

Kirby and Loretta.

Willow had been so busy with the tour group that she hadn't had time to think about them yet.

But now she did.

She thought about them leaving.

She thought about how quiet it was going to be without Kirby bouncing out there on the diving board.

Boing. Boing. Boing.

She thought about how boring it would be without Loretta skipping around in her cowboy vest.

She thought about sitting in the bottom of the swimming pool without anyone to talk pig Latin to or do yo-yo tricks with.

And then her father came into the office and she remembered what she had to do.

She stood up straight and squared her shoulders and said, "Daddy, Aggie can't leave. We need her to help us in the motel and our family got all messed up so now she can help make a family for us and we'll still have plenty of rooms for guests. Ugly won't like it in a condominium and he can't even go outside or anything."

She stopped to take a breath.

And then she said, "And Harold is in the tomato garden."

She took another breath. "Well, not *Harold* Harold, but,

you know"—she jerked her head and glanced up at the ceiling—"Harold."

There.

Willow waited.

Her father took off his cap and scratched his head. He put his cap back on and glanced up at the ceiling. Then he looked at Willow and said, "Okay."

Aggie plopped into Harold's old lounge chair. Her back hurt. That bursitis in her shoulder was acting up again. And the arthritis in her knees was interfering with the day, that was for sure.

But what a day it had been.

Just like the old days.

Well, almost . . .

"Aggie?" Willow called through the curtain over the office door.

Aggie forgot about her back and her shoulder and her knees.

"Come on in, sweetheart," she called.

Willow came in and sat on the bed in front of her. She looked so solemn, Aggie felt scared for a minute, like maybe she was about to get some real bad news.

But instead of telling her bad news, Willow said, "We need you to stay."

"Stay?"

Willow nodded. "Stay here. With us."

And then the words came tumbling out and Aggie had to lean forward a little to make sure she was hearing everything right.

This is what Willow told her:

That she and her daddy needed Aggie to help them run the motel because Willow would be going to school soon and somebody needed to be in the office while her daddy worked on other things, like weeding and filling the soda machine and checking for wasps under the eaves.

That Willow's family had gotten a little messed up and if Aggie stayed, well, maybe they could all be like a family right here at the motel.

That Ugly needed to be outside because that's what cats like, not condominiums and hot tubs.

That when Dorothy comes to visit, she will want to meet Aggie.

And that Willow and Aggie could fix up the garden together—weeding and pruning and planting—while they talked to Harold.

And then she stopped.

And Aggie said, "Okay."

"Hurry up, Kirby. I haven't got all day," Kirby's mother hollered out of the car window.

Kirby jabbed at the gravel with the toe of his sneaker.

Aggie and Willow and Mr. Dover and Loretta and her parents were gathered around him.

Loretta's parents told him how nice it was to meet him and maybe they could all go fishing next time they were out this way.

Mr. Dover thanked him for helping with the weeding and all. He couldn't have done it without him.

Aggie told him he was a fine young man and she would send him banana bread. "And you come on down here and visit us when you have some time off from school," she added.

Willow looked down at her feet and said, "Bye," with a little flap of her hand.

Loretta said, "Ee-say ou-yay ater-lay, irby-Kay."

And Ugly purred.

Kirby gave Willow his purple yo-yo.

Willow said, "Thank you."

Then he reached in his pocket and took out the poodle dog pin and handed it to Loretta and said, "Here."

He waited for everyone to yell at him.

He waited for everyone to hate him.

But Loretta grabbed the pin and squealed, "My pin! My pin! You found my pin!"

She did a little la-la-la dance around and around in circles, jangling her charm bracelet and kissing her pin.

Then she took the sheriff's badge off her fringed leather vest and handed it to Kirby.

"Here, you have this," she said.

Kirby took the sheriff's badge from Loretta and started to put it in his pocket. But then he changed his mind. "Thanks," he said, and pinned the badge to his T-shirt.

When Kirby's mother honked the horn, Kirby looked around at everyone and they were all smiling at him and no one was yelling and no one was hating him.

Kirby felt as light as air, like he was going to float right up into the sky. He got in the car and waved as his mother drove out of the parking lot.

When they started up the winding road toward Smoky Mountain Boys' Academy, Kirby looked down at the trees and the mountains spread out below them, and he knew he had been wrong.

This wasn't nowhere, after all.

La la la . . .

Loretta danced around in circles, kissing her poodle dog pin as Kirby's car disappeared up the winding road.

She climbed into the van and put the pin inside her box. She was never, ever, ever, taking that stuff outside again.

Then she joined the others out in the parking lot.

"We're coming back next summer and you can go to Dollywood with us," Loretta said to Willow.

"Okay."

"We can be best friends, okay?" Loretta said.

"Okay."

Everyone hugged.

Loretta's mother hugged Mr. Dover.

Aggie hugged Loretta's father.

Loretta hugged Aggie.

Around and around the hugs went.

Finally, Loretta and her parents climbed into the van with the sandwiches and cupcakes that Aggie had packed in a brown paper bag.

"Y'all stay in touch, now," Aggie said.

Loretta and her parents said, "We will."

Aggie patted Loretta's arm resting on the open window of the van and said, "Have you decided where you're going next on that charm bracelet of yours?"

"Yep."

"Let me guess. Texas?"

"Nope." Loretta grinned out at Aggie. "O-nay ace-play," she said.

Aggie cocked her head. "No place?"

Loretta nodded. "I like it here," she said.

Then the van bounced and squeaked across the parking lot toward the road, with Loretta hanging out of the window, waving both arms.

Her charm bracelet jingle-jangled.

And her mother said, "Aren't we lucky, Marvin?"

Aggie watched the Murphys' van disappear around the curve. Willow stood beside her, clutching Kirby's purple yo-yo.

"I guess you and I better get to work," Aggie said.

She and Willow cleaned Kirby's and Loretta's rooms. They changed the sheets and put fresh towels in the bathrooms. Willow ran the vacuum. Aggie dusted.

When they were finished, Willow said, "You wanna go sit in the swimming pool?"

Aggie chuckled. "Okay."

So she sat down there by the drain with Willow and Ugly. They talked about how good everything had turned out. That tour bus parked over there by the office. Those folks sitting in lawn chairs out by their rooms, studying their complimentary maps of the Smoky Mountains.

They talked about how good things were going to be later. How Aggie was going to be in charge of the office while Willow was at school. How Willow was going to visit Dorothy in Savannah real soon. How they could all go to Dollywood with Loretta next summer. How Kirby could come visit them when he had a break from school.

When the sun started sinking below the mountains and the air grew cool, Willow helped Aggie up off the crumbling cement and they headed for the office.

Halfway there, Aggie said, "Let's skip."

So they held hands and skipped across the parking lot. Aggie's thin gray hair bounced and her glasses slid down her nose.

As she skipped, she glanced up at the sky and said, "Look at me now, Harold."

☺   ☺   ☺

Aggie and Willow sat outside the office until the sun disappeared completely behind the mountains.

Lightning bugs flickered out across the parking lot.

The motel sign glowed in the darkening sky.

And NO VACANCY flashed on and off.

On and off.